ALSO BY

ANDREA CAMILLERI

The Revolution of the Moon

THE SACCO GANG

Andrea Camilleri

THE SACCO GANG

Translated by Stephen Sartarelli

Europa
editions

Europa Editions
214 West 29th Street
New York, N.Y. 10001
www.europaeditions.com
info@europaeditions.com

Copyright © 2013 by Sellerio Editore, Palermo
First Publication 2018 by Europa Editions

Translation by Stephen Sartarelli
Original title: *La banda Sacco*
Translation copyright © 2018 by Europa Editions

Library of Congress Cataloging in Publication Data is available
ISBN 978-1-60945-423-4

Camilleri, Andrea
The Sacco Gang

Book design by Emanuele Ragnisco
www.mekkanografici.com

Cover image: Sicilian ex voto, mixed media on tin, 1854.
Milicia Sanctuary, Altavilla Milicia, Palermo

Prepress by Grafica Punto Print – Rome

Printed in the USA

CONTENTS

THE SACCO GANG

How It All Happened

I
A FAMILY'S RISE

In the late nineteenth century, Luigi Sacco is little more than a savvy, quick-witted lad working as a seasonal day laborer on farms in the countryside around Raffadali, the town of his birth. His only wealth is his youth, two strong arms, and a keen desire to work. In every other regard, he has nothing. Not even a pair of shoes.

But he is head over heels in love with a beautiful girl by the name of Antonina Randisi, a day laborer like him, who returns his affections.

The two would like to get married and have a great many children, but they are short on money, earning barely enough to stay alive and retain at least that minimum of strength necessary to work from morning till night.

Life is hard for a day laborer.

First of all, work is not constant year-round, but, as mentioned, seasonal.

This means that you work for three months for your daily half loaf of bread and sardine, and then you don't work for three months and eat nothing except, with any luck, a crust of bread and a little chicory.

Come harvest time (for almonds, fava beans, olives, grapes, wheat), the day laborers gather in an appointed place, which is usually a square in town, and wait for the overseers to show up on behalf of the landowners and "form a crew," that is, recruit a number of people, men as well as women, and take them out to the fields.

One's chances of being chosen depend entirely on the overseer, who won't always select the day laborers for their productive capacity or desire to earn the paltry pay, but rather on the basis of a whispered word from a mafioso, or a friend, or a friend of a friend. Or else he'll just make up his mind on his own, depending on whether someone is to his liking or not.

On the other hand, anyone who has ever even tried to reason with an overseer—that is, discuss the pay or the work schedule, or complain of some abuse of power or other outrage—can forget about ever being called up again. He or she might as well stay in bed and get a little extra sleep.

Work begins at the first light of day and ends at nightfall.

A break of only one hour is allowed, to eat and attend to one's needs.

But what do the day laborers eat?

A one-kilo loaf of bread with one salted sardine and one hard-boiled egg.

Here's how it goes: with the first three quarters of the loaf, one enjoys only the flavor of the sardine and the egg. With each bite of bread, the laborer licks the sardine or puts the egg in his mouth, tosses it around with his tongue, and then extracts it still whole.

The teeth come into play only with the last quarter of the loaf.

He also drinks water, which is kept cool in a jug.

Sometimes, though rarely, the owner is generous and offers a *calatina*—that is, something to go with the bread, usually consisting of a bit of caponata or a bowl of *maccu*, a porridge of fava beans cooked in water and reduced to a kind of mush, with a tiny dab of olive oil on top.

If the day's work in the field carries over to the next day, the day laborers sleep under the stars. And sometimes somebody will sing:

At night I lie beneath the sky;
the stars above become my roof;
my pillow a bitter thistle bush . . .

The luckiest, or the oldest, take refuge in a hayloft for the night.

*

One day Luigi is told that Don Agatino, an elderly, venerated grafter of pistachio trees, wants to talk to him.

It is important to know that pistachio trees are divided into male and female, and that one male tree, which Sicilians call a *scornabecco*, is enough for eight females.

Before a female tree can produce fruit, it must live for at least twelve years. But in the twelfth year, before anything else, it must be grafted, otherwise it won't produce anything.

The female tree, however, is capricious. The graft will either take on the first try, or, if it doesn't, it means the tree wishes to remain unwedded, and there's no way you can ever get it to change its mind.

Twelve years down the drain, tending a sterile tree.

Anyone who owns a pistachio grove, however, is sitting on a gold mine. The pistachio nut is very much in demand, and fetches a very high price.

An acknowledged master of the art of pistachio grafting, Don Agatino has just lost his assistant, who picked up and emigrated to America. And so he offers to teach Luigi, who he has heard is an honest, hardworking lad, the art of grafting, so he can take his place.

Luigi accepts the offer without a second thought, mostly because the pay Don Agatino is proposing is quite good and could change his life entirely.

And so he goes on to learn a new trade.

Just three months are enough for Luigi Sacco to understand all there is to know about the art of grafting, and another three months to surpass his teacher, as Don Agatino himself will honestly admit.

Shortly thereafter, the master, old and financially secure, retires, passing all of his work on to Luigi.

Luigi's fame as a miracle-working grafter who never makes a mistake spreads fast. Soon, it's no longer small pistachio groves he's called upon to graft, but veritable forests of pistachio, at Santo Stefano Quisquina, Cattolica Eraclea, and other towns in the province.

But what started out as a craft for earning a living very soon becomes for Luigi a passion with no material interest.

For a while now, to go to work, he has to pass by a pistachio grove belonging to a judge by the name of Vassallo. But it's a dead grove, because the grafters the judge had hired grafted the trees at the wrong time. Luigi, however, realizes that the grove could still be revived, and so, without telling anyone, he grafts the trees at the right moment.

Therein lies the art: intuiting just the right moment for cutting—not a day too soon or too late.

A few days later the judge's overseer runs to his boss and tells him how the pistachio grove has re-blossomed miraculously.

The judge then summons his grafters and asks which of them was the clever one. But they all admit that it wasn't them. By roundabout means, the judge learns that it was Luigi, and so he wants to meet him. He congratulates him, thanks him, and then asks him how much he owes him for his efforts.

"Nothing."

"Why not?"

"Because I did that work for my own pleasure, not on your orders."

And he won't accept so much as a cent.

At this point Luigi, thanks to his skills, has enough money to build himself a little house and finally marry his Antonina.

*

Meanwhile, however, starved as he is for work, he discovers another trade that earns well and that he can practice between one grafting job and another.

It's so strange a trade that, to hear of it, one feels immediately like laughing: flycatcher.

It was a pharmacist and owner of a pistachio grove he'd tended who made him the proposal.

"You feel like catching flies for me?"

Luigi gave him a puzzled look.

"Are you joking, sir?"

The pharmacist explained that the flies he's supposed to catch land on the leaves of elder bushes and suck them. They are very rare, and they show up in those parts only a few days a year, in April and May.

The pharmacist then led him into the room at the back of his shop and showed him a dead fly.

"This is the kind of fly you need to catch. It's called a Spanish Fly. And it's not easy to find, as I said. For every fly you bring me, I'll pay you well."

"What's it for?"

The pharmacist laughed.

"It's for making a sixty-year-old man make love like a strapping youth of twenty. We chemists make a powder out of these flies that sells for its weight in gold. But you can only take it in tiny doses, otherwise it can be deadly."

*

By dint of catching flies and grafting pistachio trees, Luigi is soon in a position to buy, on the strength of his word, a nice big plot of land, four *sarme*[1] large. It all needs to be tilled and hoed, however, as the land has not enjoyed any daily human care for years and years.

He is able to buy it on credit because the owner has great faith in Luigi's honesty.

"You can pay me in installments when you have the money."

In the meantime, Luigi and Antonina's marriage has produced five sons and one daughter. They are, in order of birth: Vincenzo, Salvatore, Giovanni, Girolamo, Filomena, and Alfonso.

As they start to grow up, the children, not the kind to take things easy, endowed as they are with a great desire to work and to get ahead in life, begin to help their father in his labors.

Now properly tilled, their land has a vineyard, an inevitable pistachio grove, and an almond orchard.

Luigi buys two donkeys and a mule.

The little house, meanwhile, has been greatly expanded. There is also now a warehouse and a stable for the animals.

*

Then, to help his father pay the installments on the land and rid him as soon as possible of his debt burden, Salvatore emigrates to the United States when still practically a child and stays there for nine years.

He works like a slave and always sends money home.

A short while later, Vincenzo leaves for Argentina, where he will stay for eight years.

---

[1] An ancient unit of measure (*salma* in Italian), varying regionally from between 1 and 4 hectares in area. (Translator's note.)

He too, following his brother Salvatore's example, sends home as much money as he can.

That leaves Giovanni, known as "Vanni," and Girolamo, to help their father work the fields. Alfonso is still too small to hold a heavy hoe in his hands.

And, besides, his father has another fate in mind for him. An ambitious one, for those times.

Luigi wants this son to study, with the support of his family and brothers, until he obtains a degree in law.

The Saccos are all barely capable of signing their own names, they do not know how to read or write, and they suffer a great deal from being practically illiterate.

In his *Memorial*, Alfonso writes that of the great mass of day laborers in his town, only one, a man of socialist ideas, could read the newspaper, ever so slowly, and the amazing thing was that the laborers all thought that this was natural and right—that is, that only "gentlemen" should be able to read and understand the newspaper.

*

When World War I breaks out, Salvatore (who has just returned from the United States), Giovanni, and Girolamo are drafted into the army and leave for the front.

As a result, Alfonso is forced to abandon his studies and go and help his father, who is now alone, since Vincenzo is still in Argentina.

But by the end of the War they're all back together, Vincenzo included. Girolamo was injured in battle, and is now considered "seriously disabled."

*

In the fields, where father and sons continue to work side

by side in perfect harmony, they build more houses, one right next to the other, and some new stables.

Three of these houses are for Vincenzo, Giovanni, and Filomena, who in the meantime have got married.

They have also built a vat for making wine.

And a great hive colony with fifty honeycombs.

And they have bought another mule, four cows, and two horses, who would go on to sire two mules a year.

Salvatore, together with a friend who knows how to run the machinery, sets up a mill in a warehouse in the center of town, which, thanks to the location, begins to earn well.

Vincenzo, aside from working as a distributor for the Socialist cooperative (the Saccos all have socialist ideas) is also a good photographer, having learned the craft in Argentina, and earns good money at it, immortalizing weddings, baptisms, and funerals.

Giovanni then gets a brilliant idea.

Transportation to the provincial capital of Girgenti (today called Agrigento) consists of an old horse-drawn coach that carries mail as well as passengers, leaving in the morning and returning in the evening. It takes half a day each way.

But there are great many people forced to stay put each day, because the coach can't carry more than eight passengers.

And so, Giovanni, not wanting to do the coach's owner a bad turn, forms a partnership with him and, along with a few other friends, buys a bus capable of making two entire round trips daily between Raffadali and Girgenti.

And since it also cooperates with the postal service, Giovanni's company receives an annual state subsidy of 20,000 lire.

Shortly thereafter, still with the same company, Giovanni buys a truck for transporting goods along the same route as the bus.

Come harvest time, however, they all go back to being farmers.

At midday and in the evenings, the family always meets back up around the same dining table, the married siblings all sitting with their spouses.

They all live in houses one right next to the other on their common land.

There is never a quarrel, never a row between them.

They are known in town for being honest, serious people who always, infallibly, honor their word.

By this point the Saccos are well off.

They had to sweat their way to get there, but they're hardly the type to enjoy their comfort and be satisfied with that.

Vanni has a few other ideas in his head. He wants to buy at least two more buses and create some new lines to other towns nearby.

*

But there was the Mafia.

II
But There Was the Mafia

Boy, was there ever!

In the early 1920s Raffadali is entirely under the rule of the Mafia, which has replaced the government in every facet of life.

The Mafia has imposed its "code of honor" on the community, which applies, of course, to those belonging to the "honorable society," but also dictates the rules of everyday behavior for regular citizens.

For example, to resolve a family dispute, one no longer turns in private to the marshal of the Carabinieri, as used to be the case, but to the Mafia boss. Who then decides, in his own way, how to solve the problem. And his judgement, once pronounced, is without appeal.

Anyone who might rebel against such a verdict almost always risks his life, because the Mafia boss's word is sacred. It is gospel, and can never be contradicted or questioned.

You can't even go to the Carabinieri to report a burglary or the theft of your livestock. You always have to inform the Mafia boss about the matter first, whereupon he will either decide to resolve the problem personally himself, or will himself grant you permission to go and talk to the Carabinieri.

The Mafia even got involved in people's private lives and would often prohibit a marriage from taking place, or stop an individual from buying a plot of land or opening a shop.

In short, the Mafia boss wore a number of different faces: one minute he was a benevolent, accommodating patriarch, the next a skilled, wise mediator, the next a harsh judge, and most often a savage executioner.

But he was always, no matter what, a ruthless extortionist.

*

Such was the way of the old Mafia—the Mafia of the great estates and countrysides.

And Raffadali is a town that lives exclusively on its farming activities. It isn't just the big landowners who have to pay the racket, but their sharecroppers as well, and even peasants owning a scrap of land no bigger than a postage stamp.

In town, shop owners and businessmen all have to bend to the racket.

At the time, the Mafia used to resort to anonymous letters, which were as ungrammatical as they were threatening, to exact the percentage they claimed was their right.

Whoever did not pay at once became the target of certain special warnings, such as seeing his harvest burnt up, his trees chopped down, or his animals' throats cut.

If, after such warnings, no concrete gestures were forthcoming —that is, if none of the requested payments were made—the Mafia would then murder a random member of the family refusing to pay.

And they would write one last letter.

And if this one, too, got no reply, then the person to whom the letter was addressed would be killed.

In Raffadali there were two Mafia bosses. One was a farm overseer by the name of Cuffaro, the other a butcher by the name of Terrazzino.

But it was rumored that there was a lawyer behind them, the real but hidden brains behind the gang.

Alfonso Sacco writes:

"Almost every family in town had been touched in some

way by the octopus. Those whose father had been killed, those whose brother, son, or husband had been eliminated; or those who'd had their livestock poached or been robbed of other possessions."

Of note in these lines is the fact that Alfonso calls the Mafia the "octopus."

At the time, there was still no television in our country, so he had no way of knowing that one day there would be a televised series on the Mafia entitled *The Octopus*.

*

Against the reigning Mafia, the Carabinieri can do precious little, if anything at all. They merely look on, powerless, as things happen. They may arrest some insignificant thief, expressly delivered up to them by the Mafia themselves, perhaps because he stole something without their permission.

The mafiosi instill fear in people, and fear generates *omertà*, the conspiracy of silence.

The local garrison, moreover, is short on soldiers, whereas a great many more carabinieri are needed.[2]

*

Seeing that the law can do nothing about them, and that the people are not up to rebelling, the Mafia redoubles its bullying.

It's no longer enough to extort money through threats and shoot-outs and murder, or slitting farm animals' throats or burning people's crops. No, now they even want to lord it over people's destinies.

And so begins a period in which the Mafia kidnaps girls to

---

[2] The Carabinieri are a policing branch of the Italian army, hence the term "garrison." (t.n.)

force them into marrying them, or sometimes only to enjoy them for a few days and then send them home, used up for-ever.

It's like back in the day when the feudal lord would occa-sionally order his bravoes to go and bring him some fresh meat.

*

The event that triggers widespread rage against the Mafia, however, occurs in 1922, at a time when the Mafia's power seems to be encountering no more opposition.

One very hot summer evening, the three Gallo kids, one boy and two girls, quite young, decide to go and sleep outside, in the farmyard.

During the night, while they're sleeping, eight armed men show up, grab one of the two sisters, and try to abduct her. The girl starts screaming and fighting, waking her brother and sis-ter. These two immediately realize what's happening and throw themselves, defenseless, at the kidnappers, trying to rescue their sister.

They don't even have time to get close before they are ruth-lessly shot dead.

The bodies of the two young people, a brother and sister not even twenty years old, are found the next morning at dawn by their mother, who'd gone out, as usual, to work the fields.

A few days later the girl who was kidnapped is found aban-doned outside of town, just past the first houses.

But the fact of having witnessed the murder of her brother and sister, and of having suffered what the kidnappers put her through, has driven her completely out of her mind. And she will never recover. She will spend the rest of her life locked up in an insane asylum.

But that's not the end of the horror to this story.

The outrage of all the law-abiding townsfolk prompts the Carabinieri to conduct a serious investigation. And all eight of the men who took part in the kidnapping, who turn out to be sons of mafiosi, are arrested.

At the end of the trial, however, the sentence given the kidnappers is so benign—just a few months in jail—that the poor mother of the victims, a widow bereft of two children and with her only remaining child now insane, stands up to protest, only to fall back down, dead from a heart attack, in front of the judge.

*

"Nobody felt safe to go out of the house any longer," Alfonso writes about those years.

This was not an exaggeration.

III
THE FIRST DARK CLOUDS

In the first months of 1920, the Sacco family's life changes. Luigi has taught his family a precise rule to live by.

Every morning, the small table in the first room of the country house must be set and a loaf of fresh bread, a round of cheese, a variety of fruit, and a flask of wine must be laid out.

This is made available to anyone who might be passing by and needs a bite to eat and something to drink.

Whoever so wishes can come in, sit down, eat, drink, and be on their way.

No questions asked.

In addition, just outside the entrance door are some bundles of sticks for anyone who might need to make a fire.

And there are also two or three chests full of a variety of seeds, for anyone who may wish to sow them but lacks the money to buy them.

Luigi has also made it clear that anyone who comes begging for alms must be given something. And if anyone needs a small loan, that too must be granted, without interest and without fixing a date for repayment.

But it's not alms the Mafia wants.

*

One dark day Luigi Sacco receives a letter from the Mafia, demanding a large sum of money. Since he never went to school, he asks someone who'd been through the elementary grades to read it for him. But even before the person starts reading, he already knows what it's about.

That same evening, with the whole family gathered round the fire because it's cold outside, Luigi takes the letter out of his pocket and hands it to Alfonso.

"Read it."

His son reads it aloud. Luigi then takes it out of his hands and, without saying a word, throws it into the fire.

The gesture serves as a kind of pledge they all have taken at that moment: Never give in.

They never answer the letter.

Five nights later, the Saccos are woken up in the middle of the night by some loud noises in the stables.

Someone is clearly trying to steal the animals.

They all run out of their houses at the same time, firing guns in the air, forcing the thieves to flee.

First thing the following morning, Luigi Sacco pays a visit to the marshal of the Carabinieri and reports the attempted robbery.

The marshal looks at him in bewilderment.

"Are you sure you want to file this report?"

"Yes, sir, I am."

"Do you realize it's useless? That we can't do anything?"

"Well, I'm going to file the report just the same."

As Luigi is leaving the compound to get his mule, a man passes close to him and says in a low voice:

"Wrong move."

*

Less than a week later, a second threatening letter arrives and, like the first, it too receives no reply.

A few more days pass, and then some strangers set fire to

two farm buildings, one for storing food stocks for the animals, the other for all their farming tools and machinery.

The following morning, a terrified Luigi Sacco goes to the Carabinieri compound to report the crime in due fashion.

On his way to the compound, not one person he passes on the street deigns to greet him. They pretend not to see him. They want nothing to do with someone who, rather than turn to the Mafia boss to seek justice, goes to the forces of the law to report a crime.

Luigi is throwing the rules dictated by the Mafia, and obeyed by all, out the window. Luigi is practically a dead man walking.

Even the marshal of the Carabinieri, seeing Luigi appear before him, feels uneasy.

Each new crime reported by Luigi Sacco underscores, in the eyes of the townsfolk, the powerlessness of law enforcement to enforce the law.

Emerging from the station, Luigi runs into the same stranger again.

"You keep making the wrong move," the man says.

Luigi pretends not to hear him.

Not ten days go by before the third threatening letter arrives.

It meets the same end as the first two.

Just to be safe, however, Luigi Sacco moves his whole family out of the countryside and into town.

One Monday morning in early March 1920, Giovanni and Alfonso ride off on horseback, as they do every morning, to their country estate.

And they find all the houses and beehives burnt to the ground and still smoldering.

Incalculable damages.

So Luigi goes again to report the crime. As he's walking to the station, all around him turns as silent as the grave.

"Do you know who did it?" the marshal asks Luigi, who by this point has become one of the family at the Carabinieri post.

"Yes. I can even give you their names."

"Well, I could tell you their names, too. But names are not enough. Do you have proof?"

"No."

"Then I can't take any action."

"But you have to just the same . . . "

"Look, here's how it works. Even if you had this proof and I, at the risk of endangering my life and those of my men, went to arrest them, the investigating judge would release them in a matter of days. And they would all laugh in my face. It's already happened to me before. And I'm tired of it."

"So we're supposed to defend ourselves on our own?"

"I didn't say that."

"You didn't say it, but it's the logical conclusion of what you did say."

The marshal says nothing.

This time, upon Luigi's exiting, the stranger doesn't tell him he's made the wrong move, but threatens him outright.

"Take good care of yourself and your children."

Whereupon Luigi, without a word, sucker-punches him hard in the face.

The man falls to the ground. He wasn't expecting that kind of reaction. Luigi continues on his way.

Even Alfonso, at this point, though a minor, is granted a proper gun permit, with the proviso he must use it under his father's supervision.

With saintly patience, but boiling with rage inside, the Sacco brothers rebuild their homes.

But everything in their lives has suddenly changed.

Alfonso writes:

"Here ends our time of tranquility, our activity as honest workers; the peace of the family is over, and we enter the dark wood from which we shall never manage to emerge again. [. . .] We had to go into the countryside all armed with rifles, carbines, and pistols; as one of us led the livestock, the others would level their weapons so that no one could pass at the most dangerous points."

*

One evening in March, still in 1920, Alfonso notices in the distance, along the road to Raffadali, four human silhouettes advancing very cautiously.

Suspicious, he takes a better look through his binoculars and sees them taking cover in a cave overlooking the road.

The four men, to all appearances, are preparing an ambush. They want to catch the Saccos by surprise on their way home.

There are three Saccos present at that moment: Salvatore, Vanni, and Alfonso. One fewer than the group waiting for them.

Salvatore decides to race into town by way of a different road, so he can summon the other two brothers for help.

As he's running, he's stopped by a patrol of carabinieri under the command of none other than the marshal, who, seeing him in a state of agitation, becomes suspicious and wants to haul him into headquarters.

To avoid leaving his brothers unaided back in the countryside, he tells the marshal everything.

The officer decides to go and rescue the Sacco brothers.

And so, the Saccos and the carabinieri, side by side, surround the cave.

"Come out!"

A few rifle shots are their only reply. The Saccos and carabinieri start firing back, but in order to take cover they have to distance themselves a good ways from the grotto entrance.

At that point the four men, firing wildly in every direction, attempt an escape.

Three of them manage to escape, while a fourth is nabbed by the carabinieri.

Alfonso is greatly affected by this. His brothers had already fought in the war; for him this was a baptism by fire.

To their great astonishment, the Saccos recognize the man arrested as a neighbor of theirs, a certain Pasquale Manno, a former convict who had been twice wounded in attacks by unknown parties, but who had always behaved decently with them. They thought he was a friend.

Indeed, Alfonso writes that "he had very often sat down at our table."

At the Carabinieri compound, it doesn't take long for Manno to spit out the names of his accomplices: Francesco Ferro, Stefano Cuffaro, and a guy known as "Picareddra"—all Mafia grunts, all with criminal records for brawling, burglary, armed assault, and attempted murder.

*

Oddly enough, the trial begins only a few months after the event.

Pasquale Manno admits to waiting in ambush, with his friends, for the Saccos to pass along that road.

"Were you going to kill them?"

"Of course not!"

"Then why were you lying in wait for them?"

"Just to scare them, not to kill them."

"And why did you want to frighten them?"

"Because I couldn't take any more of the Sacco brothers' tyranny and bullying!"

"Why, what did they do?"

"They would come into my field and demand food and drink. And then they would even take a lamb and roast it. Another time Alfonso pointed a shotgun in my face and wanted all the money

I had in my pockets. Another time Vanni shot at me but missed."

"But do you have witnesses to what you're asserting?"

"Of course I do, your honor! Ciccio Ferro was there when Alfonso pointed the shotgun at me, and Stefanu Cuffaro was there when Vanni shot at me."

When questioned by the judge, the Saccos stammer, get confused, say the wrong things.

The fact is that they feel utterly at a loss. The deck has been stacked so brazenly that they don't know what to do.

"But didn't you see that the carabinieri were with the Saccos?"

"It was too dark," Manno blithely replies.

The whole thing is a farce, a day at the puppet theatre.

It becomes clear that Manno and his men have been reassured that they will not be convicted.

Apparently, the judges had been "spoken to."

And, indeed, the culprits are all acquitted. Their explanations are taken at face value.

And since the explanations of their enemies are taken as valid, the Saccos now expect the trial to be turned against them, making them no longer the accusers but the accused.

The judges, however, are not up to going that far.

They gather their papers, stand up, and leave.

And that's that.

IV
FIRST BLOOD

By this point the Saccos know that the Mafia has declared war on them, a war involving not just rifle blasts but also bureaucratic blows: false accusations supported by testimonies even falser than the accusations.

By hook or by crook, dead or alive, they have to be eliminated.

Their continued presence in town is a daily humiliation, an intolerable offense to the "men of honor."

The Mafia can ambush them whenever it sees fit, at any hour of the day or night; and the Saccos, for their part, can hardly stay holed up at home all the time, just to avoid danger. They have no choice but to go to their places of work, both in town and in the countryside.

On top of this, given the actions of Manno—whom they had considered a good neighbor and a sincere friend—they realize they can no longer trust anyone. They can only count on members of their immediate family.

And so they come up with a defense strategy conceived specifically for getting about daily and working in the fields.

None of them must ever go around alone. There must always be at least two of them, armed to the teeth, so that the one can always cover the other's back.

When necessary, they can request reinforcements from another brother or relative, or trusted friend.

*

But they can't possibly dodge every ambush in the nick of time.

It is Carnival, 1921. A Wednesday.

Vanni and Alfonso, who've gone to a nearby town that is hosting a livestock fair, are on their way home to their country house with the mules and horses they've just bought.

With them is their ten-year-old nephew, Luigino. The boy is tremendously pleased because his uncles showed him a good time at the fair and bought him sweets, doughnuts, and nougat.

The Saccos are traveling along a road they don't know very well, and therefore proceed in defensive formation.

They have Luigino ride on the back of a mare, while Alfonso, revolver in hand, rides a mule to which they've hitched the other mules and horses they've just purchased.

Giovanni, on the other hand, advances on foot along the land beside the road, a '91 Carcano slung over his shoulder.

Thus armed and arrayed, they look like soldiers on a reconnaissance patrol, when in fact they are peaceful, law-abiding citizens of a government unable to protect them from organized crime.

All at once someone begins firing at them from behind a dense clump of prickly pear on a slope above the road.

Falling quickly to the ground, Giovanni starts returning fire.

Alfonso, having leapt nimbly down from his mule, also begins firing wildly.

Terrified by the shots, the mare carrying Luigino starts galloping wildly away, as the little boy cries desperately, gripping the saddle with both hands.

Vanni and Alfonso lose sight of him, but they now feel less worried because the horse, all things considered, has managed to take the boy out of the range of the bullets.

As the shoot-out continues, some unexpected help arrives.

It's their brother, Salvatore, who had hopped on a horse

and rode out of town to join his brothers and lend them a hand in moving the animals.

Salvatore, in fact, finds himself in an advantageous position—that is, behind the attackers.

Without batting an eye, he starts shooting.

At this point the attackers, realizing they're practically surrounded, drop everything and run away.

The three brothers are unharmed and so start looking immediately for the little boy, whose cries and weeping are no longer audible.

They find him soon enough, unconscious on the ground, in a pool of blood.

Bounced from the saddle, Luigino had fallen, striking his head sharply against a boulder at the side of the road.

The fall will cost him his eyesight.

He will remain blind for the rest of his life.

He is the first innocent victim.

This only strengthens the Saccos' resolve. They now have one more reason never to give in to the Mafia.

*

Less than three days later, on Saturday evening, when returning to town on horseback from the countryside, holding his five-year-old son in front of him in the same saddle, Carmelo Gambino, Vanni Sacco's brother-in-law, is shot twice and falls dead to the ground.

Since Carmelo Gambino was known by all as a man with a heart of gold who had no enemies and minded his own business, everyone in town is at first convinced that the murder was an act of indirect vengeance against the Saccos.

But this isn't the case.

It's much subtler than that.

In fact, a few days later, the Saccos are informed by the

Carabinieri that they must immediately present themselves at the station.

All five?

All five.

The marshal wants them to tell him where they were on the evening Gambino was killed.

Questioned one by one and kept separate from one another the whole time, to prevent them from communicating, the Saccos all give the same exact answer.

That evening, they, along with a great many friends, were all at the home of an aunt of theirs, just outside of town.

And this can be attested not only by the people who were with them, but also by the many who saw them on their way there and exchanged a few words with them.

To get to the spot where Gambino was murdered from that aunt's house, it would take a good hour and a half on horseback.

It's an ironclad alibi.

The marshal is convinced the Sacco brothers had nothing whatsoever to do with the killing.

"All right, you can go."

"Wait a second," says Vanni. "There's something you have to tell us."

"And what's that?"

"Who told you that we were the ones who killed Carmelo?"

"An anonymous letter," the marshal replied.

And he shows it to him.

This confirms the Saccos' suspicion that the Mafia will seek another means through which to force them to surrender: setting the justice system in motion against them, charging them with crimes they never committed.

It's an intelligent strategy that was certainly not the brainchild of the local Mafia boss, who's just a coarse, ferocious killer. Behind the move it's not hard to surmise the mind of the famous lawyer who serves as the mafiosi's guide and inspiration.

Alfonso comments:

"That day at the Carabinieri office we realized they wanted to get rid of us in any way possible: either with rifles or with the law. What else could we expect now?" Salvatore, meanwhile, with great courage and much patience, has managed to find out the names of those who, on that Carnival Wednesday, laid the ambush that led to the blinding of poor little Luigino.

And to the Carabinieri he brings not only their names, but a good deal of proof so solid that the three attackers are immediately arrested.

That's when the Mafia (it's becoming clearer and clearer that they are implementing a specific scheme hatched by the lawyer) decide to play their winning card.

*

On the seventh of May 1922, Giovanni and Alfonso go to the Carabinieri compound to see if Alfonso's new gun license has arrived. By now the family's youngest has come of age, and he no longer needs the permit subject to his father's approval.

Just as they are entering the building, right in the doorway, they run into the marshal and another officer.

"What a coincidence!" the marshal says to Giovanni. "I was just on my way to your house!"

"But now I'm here. What did you want?"

"Come with me."

He leads him into his office and tells Alfonso to wait in the hallway.

Inside the marshal's office Vanni finds another man, a peasant with a beret on his head.

His name is Giuseppe Nicosia, and he has a prior record of conviction for theft and attempted murder.

Vanni, who knows the man only by sight, first thinks the marshal is going to dismiss Nicosia so he can speak alone with him. But the peasant remains seated, casting hostile glances at Giovanni.

The marshal sits down behind his desk and begins talking.

He informs Vanni that Nicosia came there to tell him that the previous night, five people—one, the leader, dressed in civilian clothes and the others disguised as municipal police—burst into his home in the country and stole three cows and one donkey.

Nicosia says he tried to react, but the leader, the one dressed in civvies, whose face was also hidden, struck him violently in the head with the butt of his rifle.

In so doing, the man's bandana fell from his face, and Nicosia was able to recognize him.

"Why are you telling me this?" asks Vanni.

"Because you were the masked man who injured me!" Nicosia shouts at him.

A cudgel blow to the head would have had less effect on Vanni.

But he recovers at once and keeps his cool, because he realizes that this time the trap that has been laid for him is extremely dangerous. He reacts quite calmly, and with straightforward logic.

First, he asks the marshal to order Nicosia to remove the cap from his head, so they can see the marks of the violence he claims he was subjected to. But the peasant promptly changes his story, saying he was struck not in the head but on the shoulder.

Giovanni then points out an inconsistency in the man's version of things. If his bandana fell from his face and Nicosia recognized him, how come he, Vanni, didn't just kill the guy to prevent him from reporting him?

The peasant sputters an explanation, claiming wildly that

Vanni did indeed shoot at him but missed, allowing him the time he needed to escape.

Vanni then turns directly to the marshal.

He asks what interest he could possibly have in going and stealing three cows and one donkey.

He's a rich landowner and has all the cows and donkeys he needs.

But it's no use.

Nicosia swears up and down that he's telling the truth.

Vanni, at this point, sees red, bolts out of his chair, grabs Nicosia, and starts punching him in the face.

With some effort, the marshal manages to restrain him.

Moments later, a bewildered Alfonso sees Giovanni come out of the office in handcuffs, flanked by two carabinieri.

The marshal calls him at once into his office.

He explains to Alfonso what his brother is accused of, but makes it clear that he doesn't believe the accusation.

And, as if to confirm his skepticism, he takes from a drawer of his desk the revolver he'd just confiscated from Giovanni and turns it over to Alfonso, along with his new gun permit.

*

At this point Luigi, the paterfamilias, seeing that the matter is quite serious and threatens to sully the family's good name, hires two of the most famous criminal lawyers of the time to defend Vanni.

One is none other than Angelo Abisso, a prince of the courtroom, a well-known, dogged representative of the Fascist movement and a future deputy in Parliament, who agrees without hesitation to defend Vanni.

Vanni, moreover, has meanwhile revealed to the investigating magistrate the names of the two witnesses who were with him at the exact moment Nicosia claims he was assaulted.

The first is named Salvatore Tuttolomondo, a wealthy peasant who had gone to talk to him about renting a portion of the
land of the Baron Spoto.

The second is Luigi Macedonio, a partner of Vanni's in the
company that owns the Raffadali-Girgenti line, who was at
Vanni's house that evening to discuss raising the bus fare.

Both are men with clean records whose testimony would
clearly help tip the scales in Vanni's favor.

It all seems off to the best possible start when some incred-
ible things begin to happen.

Tuttolomondo, the first witness for the defense, is murdered on his way back into town from the countryside where
he works.

Three days later, Luigi Macedonio, the second witness, is
shot dead in the central square of Raffadali.

And so Vanni is deprived of his principal witnesses.

Then, inexplicably, or perhaps all too explicably, the two
lawyers fail to show up on the day of the hearing.

Clearly somebody has persuaded them to drop the case.

Abisso was a frontline Fascist, and no doubt the mafiosi
turned to their Fascist cronies to persuade Abisso to stay
home, claiming illness, rather than show up at the hearing.

In addition, the two lawyers never return the formidable
advances Luigi had paid out to them.

Alfonso notes:

"At least poor Renzo Tramaglino got his four capons back
through the efforts of Quibbleweaver the lawyer, who realized
he was dealing with the bravoes of Don Rodrigo.[3] And yet all
across Italy so many lawyers still protect the Don Rodrigos
more than their poor victims!"

---

[3] A reference to a situation in Alessandro Manzoni's 19th-century novel,
The Betrothed. (t.n.)

In the end, Giovanni is convicted of armed robbery and sent to the Girgenti prison.

Only him, though, because his four accomplices were never identified, for the simple reason that they never existed.

The Mafia, this time, managed to play their cards well.

*

And, flush with their courtroom victory, they have the nerve to write another letter to old Luigi.

Aren't you getting tired of everything that's been happening to you? the Mafia ask him.

When will you make up your mind to take the more moderate path, so this time we won't have to kill someone from your immediate family? This will be our last message. From now on you would do best to seek us out yourself.

This letter, too, like the previous ones, receives no reply.

Alfonso writes:

"With my brother Giovanni now out of the way, our enemies think they will bend us more easily to their will; but we carry on working our land as before, taking the same precautions."

And these precautions will enable the Saccos, who have acquired the instincts of hunted animals, to thwart two ambushes before they could turn into firefights.

But it's a life that can't go on for long.

One can't work the earth as if going to war.

Two Mysteries: The Father's Death and Giovanni's Escape

Some time later, Vanni Sacco is transferred from Girgenti Prison to the one in Aragona.

Aragona is much closer to Raffadali, and so family members are now able to visit regularly every Sunday, as the law allows.

But there's a rather big problem . . .

The road that leads out of Raffadali in the direction of Aragona is such that it presents the Mafia with a number of possibilities for laying ambushes, and the Sacco brothers don't feel much like traveling that road on the appointed days and times.

Knowing the day and the hour in which the Saccos will set out, and the route they will be forced to take, the Mafia can easily lie in wait for them and finish them off.

The family are, however, intent on making sure their imprisoned brother still feels their warmth and presence. Vanni is a strong man, but the injustice to which he has fallen victim has very nearly made him ill.

The Saccos hold a family meeting, at the conclusion of which they decide that the person who will go and visit Vanni in prison every Sunday morning will be the head of the family, Luigi.

He's seventy-two years old at this point. Who would ever want to harm him? Anyway, doesn't the Mafia code of honor oblige them to respect the elderly, women, and children?

And so, every Sunday morning, Luigi heads out on horseback

for Aragona and returns to Raffadali around noontime, after speaking with Vanni in jail.

*

One afternoon in late May 1923, Salvatore and Alfonso, while working the fields despite the fact that it's a Sunday, look up to see a peasant they know, a certain Tabone, rushing towards them. In tears, he tells them that their father, on his way back from Aragona, was seen lying on the ground outside the gates of town, having fallen from his horse.

Vincenzo, meanwhile, is informed by some other peasants while relaxing in a café in Raffadali, and rushes to the scene with a friend to see what's happened.

Arriving there before Salvatore and Alfonso, Vincenzo finds his father unconscious and can't tell whether he's alive or dead, though he has no visible injury.

His first impression is that his father has fallen from his horse.

With the friend's help, he takes him to their home in town and immediately calls a doctor.

But the physician can do nothing but affirm that he is looking at a corpse.

"But what did our father die of?" Alfonso asks for all of them.

"Natural causes."

And he begins writing a notification of death by cardiac arrest.

Flustered by what the doctor has just said, Salvatore points out to him that this is all very strange, given the fact that their father had never been sick and, indeed, after undergoing a medical exam barely a month before by another doctor, the latter had been pleased to find him in good health and with a heart that worked like a clock despite his advanced age.

The doctor only shrugs by way of reply. To him it looks like an utterly natural death, and there is little to discuss.

Meanwhile, however, the three brothers exchange glances, asking one another in silence, with only their eyes, what that horrible bluish swelling forming under their father's chin, all around his neck, could mean.

And together, still with their eyes, they all give each other the same answer: it's a clear sign that their father was strangled.

It must have taken three men, at the very least, to kill him: two to hold him down, since the old man was still a tall, hearty, strong specimen, and another to wring his neck with both hands.

But the brothers choose to remain silent. They don't raise any questions or doubts, and accept the doctor's report without protest.

After they're left alone with their father, they have a better look at him. And if they had any remaining doubt as to how their father was killed, this is now dispelled.

*

But why did the Mafia have Luigi strangled instead of gunning him down?

And why, by murdering Luigi—that is, an old man of seventy-two—did they violate their own code of honor, which until now they'd always respected?

Had they shot him, it would have been clear to everyone that he had been murdered. And the local Mafia would have lost credibility in the eyes of the population for not obeying their own rules.

By strangling him, there was a chance the death would be judged to be from natural causes and therefore not make too many waves.

Was the doctor in cahoots with the Mafia? Or was he simply

someone who didn't know his profession very well? Whatever the case, he ended up doing what the Mafia wanted.

*

But the Mafia didn't only want to cover up that it had murdered Luigi, making him pay with his life for his firm, courageous refusal to bend to their will; they had another purpose, perhaps the main one.

With Luigi gone, his brothers would now have to be the ones to visit Vanni in jail. And they would be easy targets for the mafiosi lying in wait along the Raffadali-Aragona road.

This was the second reason Luigi was killed.

*

How, then, will they maintain weekly contact with Vanni, who is the brains, the unquestioned head of the family, especially now that Luigi is dead?

While they're discussing this question, the news that Luigi Sacco was strangled reaches the prison of Aragona, where Vanni, his son, can do nothing but weep in grief and powerlessness.

*

One afternoon, Vanni, sitting on the floor in a corner of his cell, head in his hands, looks up by chance and has the impression that the guard, having come by a short while earlier to check the solidity of the window bars, forgot to lock the cell door properly. Taking a closer look, he realizes in astonishment that the door is actually ajar!

But he decides to remain seated on the floor, as if he hasn't noticed the oddity.

He senses that there's something going on, and this disturbs him.

In fact, an unnatural silence reigns over the whole prison.

It's as if all the other inmates in the same cellblock were made to leave their cells and taken to another place.

Vanni immediately suspects a ruse, a trap being laid to eliminate him.

He thinks there must be someone lying in wait behind the door, who, upon seeing him come out of his cell, will shoot him in the back.

Hiding behind this invitation to escape is surely a murder plot. Having dealt with his father, the Mafia now wants to get rid of him too.

And all the other inmates were taken somewhere else so they couldn't become troublesome witnesses.

After a while, however, he can no longer refrain from taking action. The invitation of that door needing only the slightest of pushes to swing open is impossible to resist.

He stands up, goes over to the door, opens it ever so slowly, one millimeter at a time, until it's wide open. He feels himself drenched in sweat.

There's nobody in the hallway. The other cells are all empty.

He proceeds to the end of the hall, where there's a great barred gate. But this too is ajar!

And hanging between a couple of bars are his clothes!

He puts them on, descends one flight of stairs, at the bottom of which there's another barred gate, which opens as soon as he lays his hand on it.

A large courtyard beckons before him.

There's not a living soul about. Vanni decides to cross the courtyard slowly, one step at a time, as in a dream, waiting to be shot in the back at any moment and fall facedown to the ground, dead.

At the far end of the courtyard is another barred gate beyond which is an open lobby, where there are usually a couple of prison guards posted.

This time there's nobody.

Vanni now comes to the great main door of the prison, which looks as if it's carefully bolted.

His heart sinks. If the main door is locked, it means the whole thing was a dirty trick and that moments later the guards and other inmates will all suddenly appear and laugh at him.

But at once he notices that from the small door cut into one the great wings of the main door, there's a thread of light filtering in.

He pushes the small door just enough to open it, and suddenly finds himself outside the prison.

Not a guard in sight.

Vanni puts his hands in his pockets and even finds a few coins in them.

He's free!

He heads on foot for Raffadali.

*

This is Vanni's account of his escape from prison. His brother Alfonso gives a different version of the story. He describes a classic textbook prison break. Perhaps he does so to protect the prison personnel—and there must have been a great many of them—who got together to make his brother's getaway possible.

"That morning the jailor, with the help of the Carabinieri, had the stonemasons repair a window in the cell suite where my brother was staying. They were replacing an iron grate. At midday, they took a break from work to go and have lunch, leaving the window unbarred and unguarded, since, according to the Carabinieri's judgment, the window was too high for anybody to get out. But a bird will do all it can to escape its cage, and somehow a man is supposed to remain inside with an open door in front of him? And so, my brother, along with two other young men, climbed to the height of the window and escaped into the bright light of noon."

*

At dawn on the morning after the getaway, Alfonso and Salvatore, sleeping together in a room above the stable, are awakened by some very faint tapping at the door.

They think twice before going to open the door.

It might be a Mafia trick.

The knocking continues.

And so they grab their weapons and Salvatore goes to answer, while Alfonso, staying hidden, levels his gun at the door.

A moment later, dropping their weapons, they run and embrace Vanni.

Their brother, however, fearing the Carabinieri might be tailing him, stays at the house only long enough to wash himself and eat.

Then, after equipping himself with provisions, the '91 Carcano, and a revolver, he hugs his brothers and heads towards the Palombaia mountain, which he knows as well as the insides of his pockets.

He's the family's first fugitive from justice.

VI
THE COMPULSORY FUGITIVE

Alfonso and Salvatore are working in the fields.

It's early June, less than a week since Vanni took to the Palombaia mountain to hide out.

In the intense heat, the two brothers hear a long whistle that breaks off abruptly, followed by two short whistles.

This is the pre-arranged signal.

The person whistling is a friend who stands guard atop a small hill from which one can see the trail. He's signaling that someone is approaching.

The two brothers run to get their weapons, which they always keep within reach, hidden under a bundle of hay, but find themselves suddenly surrounded by eight carabinieri, four on foot and four on horseback, under the command of the usual marshal.

Alfonso and Salvatore immediately put the weapons back under the hay.

The marshal stands idly by, doffing his cap and wiping the sweat from his brow.

Alfonso and Salvatore pretend to be perplexed to see him, as if wondering why he's there, whereas they know perfectly well what the marshal is about to ask them.

Indeed:

"Do you know where your brother Giovanni is?"

"Yessir," Alfonso replies promptly.

"Then tell me."

"He's in jail, in Aragona," says Alfonso.

Which is in fact where he's supposed to be.

It's clearly absurd, but, if one really thinks about it, Alfonso could not have answered any other way.

There was never any official announcement of the prison break, no orders issued in connection with it. There's not even any mention of it in the prison documents.

The marshal, who learned of the escape indirectly, has gone out in search of a fugitive who theoretically cannot be a fugitive because, since he cannot be shown to have escaped, he must still be in jail.

"Don't you know he's at large?"

"How can he be at large if he's in prison?"

The marshal, however, is not pleased.

"All right, Alfonso, if you don't convince Vanni to turn himself in within three days' time, I'll revoke your gun permit."

Alfonso flies off the handle.

"Oh, no you don't! You know damn well that we can't come out to the country unarmed! It's a death sentence!"

"Then you'll have to stop coming out to the country."

Alfonso begins to see red.

"Are you kidding me? We can't just drop everything out here. And those guys'll kill us as soon as they find out we're unarmed! I swear, the day you take away our gun permits, I'm going straight up the mountain to keep my brother company!"

"Suit yourself," says the marshal.

Three days later, punctual as ever, he returns and makes Alfonso return the permit.

"You've been warned. As of this moment, if I find you carrying a weapon, I'm going to arrest you."

"Can you tell me at least why you're revoking my right?" Alfonso asks him.

"First of all, because you're the brother of a fugitive, and secondly, because you refuse to cooperate with the law."

"Then why haven't you revoked Peppe Panarisi's license?

His brother is a fugitive from the law after killing a marshal of the Carabinieri, one of your own! He's not co-operating with you either. And yet he still goes around with a gun and with your approval! Whereas my brother Vanni has never killed anyone!"

"I have my orders," the marshal says, by way of justification.

"From whom?" Alfonso asks.

The marshal looks at him and says nothing.

The fact is that Fascism has been in power in Italy for almost a year now. And the Fascists of Raffadali don't like the idea of Vanni Sacco the Socialist going around the countryside free and armed.

*

And that very day, just as he promised, Alfonso grabs his rifle and revolver and goes up the mountain to join Vanni.

Alfonso pointedly comments in sadness:

"That was how I became a fugitive: not for armed robbery or murder, but by the will of a guardian of the law."

A compulsory fugitive, like a soldier conscripted to serve.

And so, the two brothers, with no blood whatsoever on their hands, utterly innocent of any crime, now find themselves hunted equally by the Mafia and the Carabinieri.

*

One day in mid-June, as the sun is beginning to set, Vanni and Alfonso are heading on horseback for the hut a friend has offered them as a hideout, when they happen to pass by a farmstead that looks deserted.

The front door is actually broken, hanging from its hinges, the courtyard an expanse of weeds.

The moment they enter it, however, some ten armed men on horseback burst out of the farmhouse and immediately open fire on them.

They've clearly been set up, by the very man who'd offered them refuge in the hut and who they'd believed was a true friend.

Alfonso and Vanni wildly take to their heels and under a hail of bullets manage to reach a hilltop with a few small trees, where they jump down from their horses and immediately start returning fire.

It's a massive ambush by the mafiosi, who are utterly determined to eliminate the two brothers once and for all.

At this point, however, it should be added that Vanni is a marksman without peer. If he can squarely hit a coin tossed in the air with one shot of the revolver, imagine what he can do with a Carcano!

He has never missed a shot.

And, in fact, a first shot strikes one of the assailants in the shoulder, another hobbles a poor horse, and a third, this one from Alfonso, hits one of the men in the thigh.

After thinking they'd had the game already won, the attackers, discouraged and worried about Vanni's frightening aim, withdraw.

They don't even know that Vanni and Alfonso were not shooting to kill.

*

Now, however, after the ambush, the two brothers have become convinced that simply defending themselves is not enough. They must mount a counterattack.

There's no guarantee that luck will remain on their side, as it has been so far, if they continue merely reacting and fighting back defensively.

Will this consideration eventually translate into concrete actions, or will it remain only a resolution?

Later on, the legal reality will tell one story, the Sacco brothers' reality another, completely opposite one.

But facts are facts.

Shortly after the failed ambush at the farmstead, the first Mafia boss of Raffadali is murdered.

VII
DEATH OF THE FIRST MAFIA BOSS

On July 7, 1923, shortly before the sun dips below the horizon, Giuseppe Cuffaro, farm overseer for the Baron Pasciuto, decides that it's time to return to his home in town.

He gets on his horse, adjusts the rifle he always carries with him, and heads off.

There's really no need for him to go around with a weapon, since nobody who knows him would ever try to threaten him; but it's a habit he's had since his youth, when he didn't yet enjoy the respect he has today, at the age of fifty.

It's a very hot evening, and every so often Cuffaro raises the cap on his head to run his sleeve across his brow and mop away the sweat.

A bullet from a '91 Carcano strikes him right in the middle of the forehead, as he's raising his cap for the very last time.

It was as though he himself had indicated the target to the sharpshooter.

Spooked by the shot, his horse throws him from the saddle and gallops away.

Then, a minute later, two more shots strike the lifeless body on the ground.

But they're merely shots fired in order to be certain, to make sure he'd been snuffed out.

*

When the news reaches Raffadali, it makes more noise than a bomb.

Given the present state of affairs, one killing more or less wouldn't normally make much difference. But this is another matter. The Mafia's supreme chief in the area has been snuffed out. Indeed, in the eyes of some people, the act begins to take on the appearance of sacrilege.

The man who was killed was fierce and ruthless, had a great many murders on his conscience, and kept the entire town under his control. But he could boast of having many friends both in high and low places, as well as dozens of men, just as savage as him, at his command.

His death is sure to spark cries for vengeance.

Whoever killed him can rest assured that someone will try to kill him in turn.

Therefore, to commit such an act requires tremendous courage, not to mention the confidence of knowing how to dodge the inevitable campaign of revenge.

For this reason, everybody who is anybody in town already thinks that the only man capable of doing such a thing is Vanni Sacco, who, on top of everything else, had plenty of good reasons to do it.

As soon as the crime occurs, however, Vanni and Alfonso are quick to tell everyone that they had nothing to do with it.

But when the monumental funeral for Cuffaro (with almost everyone in town attending) passes under the windows of the Saccos' house, everyone following the casket raises their eyes to look up.

The windows are all shuttered.

*

The Carabinieri share the people's convictions without the

slightest doubt. It never even crosses their minds that anyone else might have been behind the killing.

And yet a Mafia boss like Cuffaro would certainly have had plenty of enemies. A man like that, who over the course of his life did nothing but visit grief and ruin upon other people.

The Carabinieri are perfectly aware of this, but they also know that no one in town would ever have had the courage to do such a thing—nobody, that is, but the Sacco brothers.

And what a shot, the one that killed him! Right between the eyes!

Therefore, the first thing they do is arrest Salvatore, Vincenzo, and Girolamo as accessories to murder, and charge Vanni and Alfonso (the two fake fugitives) as being the material executors of the crime.

But they need proof.

Not an easy thing to find.

The only person who happened to be in the vicinity when the killing occurred is a peasant by the name of Vincenzo Galvano.

"What did you hear?"

"First one shot, then two more."

"Did you hear any shouts or cries?"

"No, sir."

"Did you see anyone?"

"Yessir. After the shots, I seen two people runnin' down the trail."

"How far away?"

"'Bout two hunnert yards."

"Did you recognize them?"

"No sir. I have trachomatous conjunctivitis."

Everybody knows that Vincenzo Galvano has problems seeing, also because he goes periodically to the eye doctor. So it's not just the typical case of someone lying to the Carabinieri.

"Can't you tell us anything more about them?"

"No sir."

Then he adds:

"But they musta been young fellers, 'cause they was runnin' fast."

The significance of these words is immediately clear to the Carabinieri.

Two young men running fast.

Aren't Vanni and Alfonso Sacco still young?

That was enough.

All five Sacco brothers are brought to justice.

Alfonso writes about their relations with Cuffaro the overseer:

"We had good relations with him. Every farmer had an interest in maintaining friendly relations with members of the Mafia, particularly the overseers, because one hoped in this way to avoid trouble. On his way back to town from the baron's domain, Cuffaro would often pass by our farmstead, and we would provide him with *suddra* grass for his horse. At the moment of harvesting wheat and other grains at his domain, he would invite many other farmers to help out, and sometimes my brother Giovanni would join their number, bringing along our mules, and help transport the harvest into town. Nobody ever dared refuse the overseer this kind of favor."

Unfortunately for Alfonso—who was a highly intelligent man who learned in prison how to read good books (from Plutarch and Dante to Settembrini and Hugo) and how to think about them—this is not a very well-chosen defense.

His account gives us a picture of an overbearing overseer who not only has them feed his horse for free, but also has Vanni harvest and transport his share of the baron's grains into town, also for free.

"We did this to avoid worse problems," writes Alfonso.

But when worse problems actually did arise, from the actions of Cuffaro and his friends, might not the memory of these abuses constitute a good further motive for eliminating the overseer?

The Saccos' trial was held in Palermo barely six months later.

But there was no substantial evidence against them.

And they were all acquitted.

This acquittal merely increased the respect and admiration the people of Raffadali felt for the Saccos. The common opinion was that they had been so clever and shrewd in their murder of Cuffaro that they had left no trace of the deed, no evidence whatsoever.

VIII

AMBUSHES, BETRAYALS, AND TRAGIC MISTAKES

After the violent death of their boss, the Raffadalese Mafia acted like a punch-drunk boxer who can only stagger and doesn't know what to do next.

The Saccos, however, are certain that this disarray won't last long, and that the boxer will recover quickly to fight more savagely than before.

This is perhaps why Salvatore decides to go into hiding himself, to lend his brothers a hand.

The three Saccos, however, no longer feel safe up on the Palombaia mountain. By now everybody knows they're hiding in some cave out there, assisted by the local peasants.

They need to go to a place still unknown to both the Mafia and the law.

They remember having given help and lodging, a few years earlier, to a young man from Aragona by the name of Giovanni, who had escaped from prison.

He's certain to repay the favor.

But they need to discover his whereabouts, because he's still a fugitive. Salvatore goes out looking for him, ultimately finds him, and brings him back.

Giovanni listens carefully to the brothers' request and immediately says he's willing to help them without reservation, just as they had once done for him.

But he says that he needs two days, at the very least, to find a place where the Saccos can stay safely.

"But where are you staying?" Vanni asks him.

"Nobody else can come where I'm staying. Here's what we'll do. If I can't find a place for you right away, I'll definitely get back in touch with you in two days' time."

Indeed, two days later, he comes back to the Sacco brothers.

With him he's brought a mule mare equipped with two *cuffuna*, large wicker baskets containing only straw inside.

He tells them he hasn't found a place yet, but that in the meantime he can put them up in a country cottage of his, just outside Aragona.

They head out.

The young man leads the way on his mule, with the three brothers following behind, though staggered at a distance from one another, guns at the ready.

At the gates of Aragona, the young man stops, gets down from his mule, and waits for Vanni to come forward ahead of the other two brothers.

"What is it?"

"You're not allowed to pass through Aragona with guns in your hands."

"When we get into town we'll put our revolvers in our pockets and our rifles on our shoulders."

"All right. But you should know that there are Carabinieri patrols in town."

Running into the Carabinieri would not be a good thing.

"What do you think we should do?"

"Put your weapons in the *cuffuna*, and I'll bury them under the straw. You can take them back out after we've passed through the town."

It's a reasonable suggestion.

But Vanni doesn't like it. By this point he simply can't go anywhere unarmed, and so he orders Salvatore and Alfonso to follow his example and keep their handguns and rifles at hand.

"Suit yourselves," the young man says with a shrug. Then

he adds: "But then we can't go down the main street of town. The Carabinieri are looking for me, too. We'll take the first road to the left."

They set out again, but the youth has his mule pull out ahead, as if he wanted to put more distance between him and the other three.

Vanni notices this and becomes suspicious.

Things are starting to seem fishy to him.

And so he whispers to his brothers the name of an owner of a farmhouse in the area, whom he knows they can trust. If anything goes wrong, they should all meet back up there.

They turn onto the street to the left. It's flanked by stone walls on both sides.

They barely have time to take a dozen steps when, all of a sudden, a deadly burst of gunfire opens up on the three of them.

They've walked into an ambush.

How many gunmen are there, anyway? Ten, twenty, thirty? Bullets are raining down from all sides.

The three brothers are not taken by surprise, however. With their suspicions aroused by the Aragonese youth's strange manner, they're able to retreat under their own wild cover of gunfire.

If they'd taken the young man's advice and disarmed, they would now be three corpses on a city street.

They meet back up late that night at the farmhouse. But it's a little too close to Aragona. The men who ambushed them may still be looking for them.

Vanni has a cut on his left arm where a bullet grazed him, but he doesn't want to waste any time dressing the wound. They have to get away from that accursed place as quickly as possible and return to their prior hideouts. There, at least, everyone was on their side.

*

One week later, the Aragonese youth who betrayed them is found dead from a rifle shot.

For the Carabinieri, there's no doubt whatsoever. The culprit is Vanni, taking revenge for the young man's betrayal.

But how—the Saccos wonder—did the Carabinieri find out that there'd been an arrangement between them and the victim, and that the youth had used the arrangement to set them up?

At first, they have no answer.

They're convinced the kid sold them to the Mafia.

And this was, in fact, the case, except that the Mafia had also invited the Carabinieri to the hunting party. So behind one wall, shooting at the Saccos, was the Mafia, and behind the other wall were the guardians of the law.

The Saccos' version of the murder is that the youth was killed by the Mafia because he'd failed in his task of persuading the brothers to put their weapons in the baskets.

*

One morning, a few days after the abortive ambush, Salvatore goes to talk to a friend, who's working in a field outside a town nearby.

On his way there, the ring linking the strap on the rifle he's holding, barrel-down, on his shoulder, suddenly breaks free, and the weapon risks falling to the ground. Without thinking, he hooks the strap's buckle onto the metal trigger guard and keeps on walking.

A short while later, as the trail becomes harder to negotiate, he stumbles on a rock, and the abrupt movement of his body causes the strap buckle to catch on the trigger.

A shot goes off and hits Salvatore squarely in the foot.

This would have been enough of a disaster in itself, in that they had to amputate one of his toes in a Palermo hospital. But

Salvatore could never have imagined that the injury would become a piece of evidence against him.

*

Less than a month goes by before two of the Saccos' cousins, Giovanni Plano and Stefano Mangione, both fathers with clean records, truly honest men and considered by all as such, lose their lives in a shoot-out.

Here's how it went.

Giovanni Plano and Stefano Mangione, who'd brought his ten-year-old son along with him, were in a group of people who'd stopped at a drinking trough to rest and have a bite to eat.

They were on their way back from Ribera, where they'd gone to sell some livestock, and so they had a tidy sum of money in their pockets.

As they're getting up to resume their return journey to Raffadali, Mangione's little boy, who's walked ahead a bit, comes running back, saying that he's seen some armed men a short distance away.

They'd signaled to him to go on and keep walking, but the boy got scared, turned tail, and ran back towards his father.

The whole group immediately think that it must be people who want to steal the proceeds from the sale of their animals, and so they begin to proceed with extreme caution, rifles in hand.

All at once Vincenzo Mangione, Stefano's brother, who's quite scared and nervous, sees some shadows appear and opens fire.

The others immediately return fire.

The two cousins also start shooting, but get the worst of the exchange.

Later it will be Vincenzo Mangione himself, crying his eyes out, who tells the Saccos what happened.

The Carabinieri, however, have meanwhile found all the money gained from the livestock sale, untouched, in the dead men's pockets. Therefore it was not a robbery.

Want to bet, they tell themselves, that the Saccos had something to do with this?

Maybe Plano and Mangiano didn't want to help the Saccos, and so the fugitives killed them.

This triggers a search of the Sacco home, and the authorities find Salvatore there, still limping from the injury to his foot.

"How did that happen?"

Salvatore can't very well tell them his rifle went off by accident, since his gun permit had been taken away some time before.

One look, however, is enough for the Carabinieri to realize that the injury was caused by a firearm.

"You got this injury when Plano and Mangione were trying in vain to defend themselves against you."

Conclusion: the double murder will end up falling on the shoulders of Salvatore, Alfonso, and Vanni.

The Saccos are unable to use Vincenzo Mangione's confession in their own defense.

On top of everything else, another of Vincenzo's brothers, Francesco, is married to Filomena, the Saccos' sister.

Despite this lack of defense, one year later, the Palermo Court for the Prosecution of Indictments sets them free.

IX
The Unfortunate Heirs

The Mafia, meanwhile, needs to find a new boss.

By rights the position ought to fall to Salvatore Terrazzino, a butcher by trade—of both animals and men—second in ferocity only to Cuffaro, who considered him his ward.

But Salvatore Terrazzino has, for some time now, been behind bars in Girgenti, awaiting a murder trial that never seems to get under way.

And so a compromise is reached.

The person to take Cuffaro's place will be Terrazzino's brother, Giovanni, former overseer of the Milone domain and a man whose capacity for murder is unquestioned, as he has already proved several times.

For the big decisions, Giovanni will act in accordance with the instructions he receives from his brother Salvatore in prison.

As soon as he assumes his new position, Terrazzino makes it known far and wide that his first task will be to kill the Saccos, who are guilty of having killed that fine, venerable gentleman, Giuseppe Cuffaro.

Giovanni Terrazzino, however, is fated to enjoy his new power for only a few months.

On the morning of January 10, 1925, the new Mafia boss is on his way back to Raffadali, in the company of his brother Domenico, after spending the night at his country house.

It is cold outside, but the sky is clear.

The two brothers are riding side by side along a trail empty of people at that hour of the morning, the peasants having already come out in the opposite direction on their way to work.

The two brothers are armed. Seeing a large bird on a tree branch, Domenico, who's an avid hunter, takes the rifle off his shoulder.

"What are you doing?"

"I want to shoot that bird."

"No. Don't make any noise."

He's a cautious man, Giovanni Terrazzino. With the Saccos, who are doggedly determined and capable of anything, the less noise one makes, the better.

Domenico, rifle still in his hands, looks again at the bird, which then flies away.

Then he hears a crisp report. Just one. And he sees his brother, Giovanni, shot in the middle of his forehead, fall from his horse.

He turns his mount and rides off, yelling in fear.

A second shot hits him from behind in the left shoulder.

But Domenico manages to remain in the saddle and ride desperately away.

*

To the marshal of the Carabinieri of Raffadali, Domenico swears up and down that he did not recognize who was doing the shooting.

"Was there only one man?"

"No, sir, there were two or three of them. Or maybe four."

"Very far away?"

"No, just a few yards."

"But if they were so close, how could you not have recognized them?"

"They had shawls over their heads."

Shawls hiding their faces, to avoid recognition.

One week later, after receiving the order from his brother Salvatore in Girgenti Prison, Domenico completely changes his story, and even starts naming names to the investigating magistrate.

"They fired at us around Portella Rognosa, and my brother Giovanni fell from his horse."

"How many of them were there?"

"Four."

"Did you recognize them?"

"Yessir."

"But didn't you tell the Carabinieri they were wearing shawls?"

"Yes, but they had the shawls wrapped around their heads, not their faces."

Then what was the point of wearing the shawls? the judge should have fired back at this point. To protect themselves from the cold?

But the magistrate said nothing about the oddity of this, and moved on to the next question.

"Can you name them?"

"Yessir. Vanni Sacco, Alfonso Sacco, Filippo Marzullo, and Pietro La Porta."

Marzullo and La Porta are two peasants who had very good reasons for becoming friends and supporters of the Saccos. Marzullo's father was murdered by the Mafia, and, as for La Porta, Salvatore Terrazzino personally killed two of his brothers, Luigi and Emmanuele.

It's a good opportunity to throw all four in jail.

"And what did you do next?"

"I raced away, with them shooting at my back. After I'd gone about six hundred yards, a shot hit me in the shoulder."

"Can you tell me why they let you get so far away before they started shooting?"

"Maybe they didn't mean to kill me."

"Why didn't you tell the Carabinieri you'd been wounded?"

"It was light stuff. Bird shot."

Another witness for the prosecution is a peasant lad by the name of Vincenzo Galvano (the same name as the other witness to the killing of Cuffaro), who was in the company of Mariano Mangione, a man well on in years.

The boy claims that right after the shoot-out, he saw Vanni and Alfonso Sacco ride by, while Mangione says that the lad is making it all up, since nobody rode past them.

Right after making his declarations to the judge, someone gives young Vincenzo Galvano, as a token of thanks, a ticket for a ship to America.

Mariano Mangione, after contradicting Galvano, ends up in Girgenti Prison, charged with being an accessory after the fact.

Incidentally: having firmly maintained his denial all the while, he is ultimately released.

In the minutes of the trial, we read that "Mangione died on August 22, 1925, as we learn from his death certificate."

Now, if we go and look at this death certificate, we discover that Mangione did not die of natural causes, as the trial papers would have us think, but was shot and killed.

While Mangione was in jail, Salvatore Terrazzino threatened to kill him if he didn't back up the Galvano boy's story. But Mangione stood firm. Therefore there was no doubt in anybody's mind that he was murdered on orders from Salvatore Terrazzino.

At any rate, the Carabinieri, the judges, and the people of Raffadali also had no doubt that the elimination of the second Mafia boss was the work of Vanni and Alfonso Sacco.

*

In one way or another, however, the Saccos' message—or what is thought to be the Saccos' message—is duly received by the right persons.

In fact, the guy who is third in the hierarchical order of the Mafia in Raffadali, and who therefore should have replaced Giovanni Terrazzino, disappears from town, literally from one day to the next: he was there the evening before and is gone the next morning.

Where did he go?

At first everyone thinks his body must be lying somewhere at the bottom of a well or at the foot of a cliff, almost surely murdered by the Sacco brothers.

Some ten days later, however, it becomes known that he went off to hide in Palermo, and that from there he took ship for the United States along with another mafioso.

They saw the way the wind was blowing and preferred the path of exile to the task of confronting the Saccos in battle. Such is the widespread belief.

And the honest people of Raffadali rejoice upon feeling the Mafia's grip on the town relax.

*

Meanwhile, however, the position of chief mafioso of Raffadali is still vacant, and there are some who covet it. But it requires great courage.

There's a guy from Santa Elisabetta, a town not far from Raffadali, by the name of Stefano Catalano, who begins speaking discreetly with low-ranking mafiosi of Raffadali, in the hopes of advancing his candidature.

But he's not even granted time to get moving.

On the evening of March 9, 1926, he's shot outside the door to his house and dies at once from the single shot.

When his wife asks him who it was, he, with his last breath, barely has time to reply:

"You know who it was."

"And do you know who it was?" the Carabinieri ask the wife.

"Vincenzo Ariosto and Giuseppe Infantino," the woman replies.

The medical examiner rules out, however, that Catalano could have had enough strength left to talk.

It's very hard to talk when one is shot between the eyes with a bullet from a '91 Carcano.

At this point Catalano's brother, Girolamo, intervenes, claiming he saw, on the same morning of the killing, at none other than Ariosto's house, Vincenzo and Girolamo Sacco, who were behaving in guarded fashion and speaking softly with him. Without wasting a minute, the Carabinieri go and arrest Ariosto and Infantino as the material executors of the crime, and Vincenzo and Girolamo Sacco as the instigators.

The whole affair, however, is fated to end up a farce.

Indeed, at the hour in which Catalano claims to have seen Girolamo Sacco at Ariosto's house, Girolamo was at Girgenti Prison talking with his brother Salvatore, who had just been arrested.

Worse yet, on the evening of the murder, Vincenzo Ariosto was in the office of the Assistant Commissioner of Police Giannitrapani, having brought a nephew of his there to turn himself in!

*

For the Saccos it's clear that behind all these maneuvers against them lurks the real brains of the Raffadalese Mafia, the highly intelligent and powerful lawyer, C.

He's the one who decides whom they have to pay, who determines the amounts, who studies the strategies to take— that is, whom to kill and whom not to kill, whose house to burn down, whom to send one last warning.

But he's able to remain in the shadows, and never comes

out into the open, even though everyone in town knows that the mafiosi do what he tells them to do.

When Attorney C. wants to go from Raffadali to his country domains, he always travels in a small two-seater carriage, a tilbury the Sicilians call a *scappacavallo*, which he drives himself.

One day, some time after lunch, the lawyer is on his way back into town, alone. He's running late, and for this reason has the whip in his hand, every so often trying to lash the horse to run.

At a certain point, while raising the whip before bringing it down on the horse's haunches, he hears a gunshot behind a clump of weeds at the side of the road.

With pinpoint accuracy, the shot snaps the whip in two, leaving only the grip in his hand.

He doesn't even have time to realize what is happening when a second shot, as precise as the first, takes his hat off.

Scared to death, and without waiting for the third shot, the one that will take his life, he starts shouting like a madman, inciting the horses to run faster.

Returning home safe and sound, the lawyer locks himself inside. He has understood the warning.

But he can't stay holed up at home forever, telling everyone he feels a little indisposed.

Sooner or later he'll have to come back out to attend to business.

And Vanni Sacco will be waiting for him.

One morning, just before dawn, the lawyer goes cautiously out of his house, looks around, takes one step, and nothing happens.

The follow day he does the same, with the same results, to the point that he feels like going out into the square.

A week later, he resumes his usual life, with his usual arrogance.

He doesn't know that Vanni is toying with him, like a cat with a mouse.

One afternoon, he brings together some ten mafiosi at his country house, to decide how to resolve the Sacco problem.

At nightfall, after the meeting has ended and three or four mounted mafiosi await him to escort him back into town, and the lawyer is locking the door, a series of rifle shots in extremely rapid succession etch his silhouette into the wooden door.

As the lawyer faints and falls to the ground, the mafiosi start firing, but in vain. They have no target and merely make a lot of noise, because the gunman is already gone.

Returning home to Raffadali more dead than alive, the lawyer buries himself in his house. He will only come back out after the Sacco brothers are caught.

But he has lost all his prestige and power.

By this point, Vanni, Alfonso, and Salvatore seem uncatchable.

The townsfolk, tickled and happy at their newfound peace with the Mafia now gone, help them in every way they can.

Not just the little people and the peasants, but even some of the "gentlemen" who used to pay the Mafia large sums of money.

The order, however, is that the Saccos must be taken, dead or alive.

Among other reasons because at this point there are some people going around saying, in this era of the March on Rome, that if all Socialists had taken action like the Sacco brothers, the Fascists would never have risen to power.

X
The Iron Prefect

Meanwhile, in 1924, Prefect Cesare Mori arrives in Sicily with precise orders from Benito Mussolini, the head of the government since 1922, to exterminate the Mafia.

This raises two questions:

Why has Mussolini decided to fight the Mafia?

And who is Cesare Mori, whom the newspapers will soon be calling "the Iron Prefect"?

*

Mussolini was led to conduct his ferocious anti-Mafia campaign for two reasons: one personal, and one involving considerations of political and economic power. It certainly was not out of a desire to abolish a system that inflicted severe damage on the social fabric of Sicily.

Politically speaking, when Fascism took power, the majority of the Mafia found itself aligned with the free-market followers of V.E. Orlando, who, in a speech given at the Teatro Massimo of Palermo in 1924, had gone so far as to proclaim proudly: "I declare myself a mafioso too!"

A minority, however, aligned themselves with the Fascists. When he became a deputy in Parliament, a famous oculist by the name of Alfredo Cucco, a former nationalist who was said to be in cahoots with the Mafia, actually became a member of the very exclusive Directory of the National Fascist Party.

During his trip to Sicily in 1924, Mussolini was publicly insulted by a powerful Mafia boss by the name of Ciccio Cuccìa—an "unspeakable" man, by Mussolini's own definition, and mayor of Piana dei Greci—and none of the authorities present had the courage to protest.

The episode is worth retelling.

After visiting Palermo, Mussolini felt like seeing a few provincial towns, including Piana dei Greci (today known as Piana degli Albanesi).

Prefect Cesare Mori, knowing that the peasants of Piana had strong Socialist traditions and that, on top of this, the town was governed by a mafioso, had Mussolini escorted by some twenty police officers on motorcycles.

When Ciccio Cuccìa went down into the square to greet the head of the government and found himself surrounded by a great many policemen, he said to the Duce, loud enough for the citizens crowding the square to hear:

"What's up with all the cops, your Excellency? When you're with me you got nothin' to fear, sir, 'cause I give the orders around here."

Then turning to the crowd, he said:

"Nobody touch a hair on Mussolini's head, 'cause he's my friend, and he's the best man in the world."

Mussolini turned green with rage.

During that journey, he also realized what the mafiosi wanted from him in exchange for their total support: "to leave power in the hands of a few hundred lowlifes," in his own words.

And so he granted Prefect Cesare Mori full powers to do as he saw fit.

*

Mori, among other things, knew Sicily well.

He'd already been there just after the War, to put down the

riots born of the disappointment of the peasantry, who had been promised, for the umpteenth time—to stoke their patriotic spirits during the conflict—their own lands for cultivation, only to see the promise broken for the umpteenth time.

Later appointed Prefect of Bologna, he was transferred by the Fascists because he'd sent dozens of them to jail after the terrible violence at Palazzo d'Accursio in 1920.

The prefect, in short, was someone who wasn't afraid of anyone.

And he was as honest a functionary as he was ruthless.

Mussolini sent him back to Sicily with vast powers.

Mori fought the Mafia by using the exact same methods as them, and by having at his disposal the Carabinieri, the police, special forces who answered only to him, and even certain sectors of the army.

"Under the pretext of fighting the Mafia, they set aside general principles of law, as well as constitutional guarantees under the Albertine Statute, the observation of *habeas corpus* for all citizens, criminal trial safeguards, and the correct application of the very statutes concerning law enforcement. Whole organs of the government, with the excuse of enforcing the law, made no bones about operating outside the law and even against the law [. . .]. They would organize veritable raids to execute arrest warrants [. . .] In a few cases, they even went so far as to besiege a whole town (the classic example being Gangi sulle Madonie) using not only the police but the army. Then, in a more general way, if they couldn't get their hands on the alleged mafiosi, they would arrest their family members— the father, a brother, sometimes even the mother or wife—to force the fugitive or fugitives to turn themselves in. [. . .] [T]he barbarous, illegal recourse to torture, using the *cassetta*[4]

---

[4] A torture method whereby a tube is thrust down the victim's throat and filled with salt water. (t.n.)

or other instruments of refined, sadistic cruelty, was not infrequent." (F. Renda, *Storia della Sicilia dal 1860 al 1970*, vol. II, Palermo 1985.)

A dictatorship can allow itself such things, and more.

*

Mori brought down such important figures of Sicilian Fascism as Alfredo Cucco and General De Giorgi, and imprisoned historic Mafia bosses such as Vito Cascio Ferro, Calogero Vizzini, and Genco Russo.

And hundreds of other mafiosi began to crowd the jails along with them.

Apparently Fascism defeated the Mafia by imposing not the law as it stood, but the law of terror.

But how is it, then, that as soon as Fascism fell, the Mafia came back stronger and more powerful than ever?

Writes Denis Mack Smith (with Moses Finley, *A History of Sicily*, 1968):

"If the Mafia had been a society rather than a way of living, perhaps Mori could have killed it for all time, but in fact its complicated social and economic causes could not be removed in this brief period or by these methods alone. Perhaps there was insufficient wish among certain people for more than a surface victory of prestige; and Vizzini and Russo were later released for 'lack of proof.'"

The classic lack of evidence, always conveniently used by judges both in democracy and under Fascism.

The prefect, moreover, had also started to annoy the Sicilian nobility, which owned the vast landed estates on which the Mafia was born and grazed. The prefect was convinced that there was some kind of arrangement between the big landowners and their mafioso overseers.

As soon as he began to make his first moves in this direction, however, he was recalled to Rome, and his career came to a halt.

The same Alfredo Cucco got his name in the papers again around 1940, mostly as the author of a book in which he claimed that coitus interruptus makes you go blind.

At any rate, for the first two years, Mori took little or no interest in the Raffadalese Mafia.

Maybe because he knew that there was already someone taking care of it.

XI
The First Attempt at Capture

When Mori finally decides to turn his attentions to the Raffadali Mafia, it makes the Sacco brothers' life much more difficult than before.

The prefect has let it be known that he has no problem turning a blind eye, and maybe even two, on anyone who, in exchange for avoiding arrest, is willing to spy and report on others.

And there are still a great many many lowlifes, low-ranking mafiosi, and friends of mafiosi around, all quite capable of selling out the Saccos in order to gain some favor in the eyes of the law.

Now the Saccos even have to beware of their own shadows.

They can no longer trust anyone.

Defying the risk of running into a patrol of the Carabinieri or special forces now teeming everywhere in and around Raffadali, Vanni and Alfonso one day are forced, by necessity, to go into town to attend to some business.

Economically speaking, they're in a pretty bad way, having had to sell most of their properties. Living as fugitives, and paying lawyers, is costly.

Being, of course, unable to go anywhere near their houses—which are under police surveillance night and day—they find shelter in a secluded cottage just outside of town and belonging to their old friend and comrade, Filippo Marzullo.

They are, as usual, armed to the teeth.

But shortly after their arrival, the cottage is suddenly surrounded by some ten carabinieri under the command of a

Sergeant Jannuzzo, who knows the Saccos well because he's been part of the Raffadali garrison for years.

Someone saw them entering that cottage and went and snitched on them. Someone who wanted to gain from having had the Saccos arrested.

Sergeant Jannuzzo orders his men not to move for any reason, and not to shoot for any reason.

Then, coming out into the open, he walks over to the clearing in front of the little house, calls Vanni's name, and, as soon as he realizes the latter is listening behind the closed shutters, he asks:

"Would you let me in, Vanni? I only want to talk to you. After all, you know as well as I do that you won't shoot me."

So saying, he lowers his carbine, takes out his revolver, and sets both down on the ground.

Ever so slowly, the door to the house opens, and the sergeant goes inside.

Meanwhile, news of the brothers' imminent capture has already spread all across Raffadali, in the twinkling of an eye. Dozens of townsfolk start running towards the house, and when they get there, the municipal cops have trouble keeping them at bay.

Inside, the sergeant has offered the two brothers cigarettes, and Vanni has returned the favor with a glass of wine.

All three are sitting calmly around a table, like friends resting after a hunting party.

The brothers' rifles are propped up in a corner.

"You have done what you felt it was your duty to do. You have avenged your father. But now the game must end. You have never shot at us, but if you continue to flee from justice, sooner or later your situation will worsen. This is inevitable. In order to avoid being caught, you will have to return our fire. And you may end up killing one of our men, at which point none of you will come out alive."

This, in so many words, is the argument the sergeant makes to them.

The logic is not only ironclad, but it touches on a sore point the Sacco brothers have been nursing for a while, even though they have never discussed it among themselves.

They've long sensed that the accursed day would eventually come when they'd have to make a choice: either shoot at the forces of order and in so doing become the criminals they've never been, or put their hands up and surrender.

That day has now come.

In fact, after less than an hour's discussion Vanni and Alfonso agree with the sergeant that there's no longer any way out for them.

And so they give themselves up to the Carabinieri.

"It's the right thing to do," says Jannuzzo.

"Will you handcuff us?" Vanni asks pointedly.

"I have no choice."

Vanni thinks about this for a moment.

"Isn't there another way to do it?"

"What would that be?"

"You leave a guard of two carabinieri outside here. That way you're assured we can't escape. This evening, after it gets dark and there are no people on the roads, Alfonso and I will come, one at a time, and turn ourselves in at the station. We don't want to suffer the humiliation of walking through the streets of town in handcuffs."

The sergeant knows that the Saccos have never, for any reason, failed to keep their word. So he asks:

"Do you give me your word of honor?"

They do.

"All right, then, it's a deal," Jannuzzo concludes, standing up.

But Vanni turns and asks him a favor.

"Could you please let our aunt, Zia Grazia, know that

we're here? And could you tell your men to let her through? If we're going to end up in jail, we'll need to talk to her."

Zia Grazia is the sister of the Saccos' mother. The brothers want to give her full power of attorney, since they'll be heading to prison.

The sergeant sends one of his men to get the Saccos' aunt and goes back to the compound with the rest of his squad, after sending away the crowd of townsfolk. As agreed, he leaves only two carabinieri on guard.

A short while later, he receives a visit from the Fascist political secretary of the town. The man is hopping mad at the sergeant, foaming at the mouth and pounding his fist on the table.

"Why didn't you arrest them? It was your duty to arrest them on the spot! I'm going to report you to your superiors! I'll send you to jail along with the Saccos!"

"Watch what you say!"

"You're their accomplice!"

Getting fed up, the sergeant threatens to throw the secretary, Fascist or not, into a holding cell.

The man pretends to calm down.

The sergeant then explains to him the agreement he made with the Saccos and says he's more than certain that they will keep their word.

But the political secretary wants instead a clamorous arrest with great pomp and drama; he wants to march the brothers past the whole population in handcuffs and make them objects of public scorn.

"We must make an example of them! We can't be granting privileges to common brigands who dare to flout the Fascist order!"

But the sergeant won't budge from his position. He, too, in a way, gave his word of honor to the Saccos.

Threatening reprisals and punishment, the political secretary leaves the compound, and from the local Casa del Fascio[5] he immediately rings Mori's headquarters in Palermo.

From Palermo, someone at headquarters rings the Raffadali Carabinieri compound in turn: the operation to arrest the Saccos must be immediately resumed, and Sergeant Jannuzzo will be replaced by a marshal at the head of a special forces unit sent from the provincial capital, Girgenti.

The Saccos' aunt barely manages to exit the house in which her two nephews are holed up before the place is encircled by some thirty special forces troopers in threatening combat gear, having rushed there from the provincial capital.

The political secretary is also there and laughing in satisfaction. The Saccos have no way out.

"Vanni and Alfonso Sacco, give yourselves up!" the marshal of the special forces orders them.

No reply.

"I'm giving you three minutes to come out with your hands up!"

No reply.

In the meantime, the hundreds of townsfolk who'd come running back to the site stand there in silence, clearly fearing for the fate of the Saccos.

The three minutes pass.

"What should we do?" the marshal asks the political secretary, whose brain is churning, thinking that by this point his career is assured.

"Start shooting," he replies.

A barrage of gunfire breaks out as if in wartime, smashing up shutters, doors, and windows, and shooting the plaster off the façade.

---

[5] The Case del Fascio were local Fascist Party headquarters established in small urban centers all over Italy. The headquarters in the big cities were called Palazzi del Littorio. (t.n.)

"Stop! Cease fire! And you, Saccos, come out!"

No reply.

"What should we do?"

"Go inside!" the political secretary orders.

With three other men, the marshal approaches the house cautiously, kicking in the already damaged door. The four men burst in.

Moments later, the marshal appears in an upstairs window.

"There's nobody here! They've escaped!"

As the townsfolk break into loud applause and mocking laughter, the marshal discovers an underground tunnel.

He bends down, goes inside, and follows the tunnel to where it comes out in the open countryside.

By now the Saccos are far away, safe and sound.

XII
DECEPTION AND REPRESSION

Oftentimes, during the long, wakeful nights standing guard over the other brothers asleep on a cave floor, every one of the Saccos has asked himself how they, as the good, honest people they were, could have ended up living like hunted animals.

On top of this, they are tired—tired of shooting, tired of fleeing, tired of life on the lam. They were not cut out for such a life; they were born simply to do honest work.

Writes Alfonso:

"We were weary of the sad, terrible life of fugitives, so full of dangers, and we understandably longed, indeed yearned, to find a way out as soon as possible, to liberate our family from the dogged, unjust persecution of Fascist law."

And so, one summer night in 1925, they talk it over amongst themselves, and decide to try and figure how they might get out of their predicament.

The richest, most important man in town is a certain Commendatore V, whose firstborn son was actually baptized by none other than His Majesty Vittorio Emanuele III in person. He is thus a crony of the king.

And not only is he a monarchist, he's a Fascist as well and has given so much money to the party that the Honorable Angelo Abisso (the same one who didn't show up at the trial) has dubbed him "the Prince of the Fascist Loan."

It is well known to all that a word from him to the judges is often enough to change the outcome of a trial.

Why not go and talk to him openly?

He must surely be aware of the facts and know that the Saccos have never done any harm to honest people.

The brothers send a friend to talk to him, and the commendatore agrees to receive them at night at his country house.

Alfonso and Vanni go to the meeting, unarmed, out of respect for the man and his house.

"What can I do for you?"

In few words Vanni tells him their story, which the commendatore says he already knows in part.

"And what do you intend to do now?" the commendatore asks when he's finished.

"We want to turn ourselves in to the authorities."

"So then why did you come to me instead of going to the Carabinieri?"

"Because we would like you to put in a good word for us."

"Meaning what?"

"To make sure we get a fair trial."

The commendatore looks at him but says nothing.

The two brothers don't know what to do. The man's silence troubles them greatly.

But when at last the commendatore decides to speak, he says something that catches them totally by surprise.

"I don't think it's such a good idea."

"What isn't?" asks Vanni.

"To turn yourselves in."

The two brothers feel lost at sea.

"Then what should we do?"

"I didn't mean you should never turn yourselves in; just not right now, because one can't reason with Mori."

"When, then?"

"I'll let you know when. And actually, only Vanni should turn himself in, because you, Alfonso, haven't done anything. When the time is right, my dear Vanni, I'll accompany you myself to the courthouse, and when it's over I'll bring you back home, acquitted of all charges."

He then stands up, sticks his hand in his pocket, pulls out two hundred and fifty lire, and hands them to Vanni, who at first doesn't want to accept the money, but in the end has no choice, so insistent is the commendatore.

Alfonso comments:

"I can still hear those words ringing in my ears. They were a great relief to us that night, a tremendous hope for our future! But neither I nor my brother was clever enough to realize just how hypocritical this character was."

Indeed the following morning the commendatore leaves for Palermo. He wants to speak personally with Mori. He intends to tell him that the people of Raffadali have had enough of the Saccos, and that the fact that they are still at large is a disgrace they cannot tolerate much longer.

His complaints fall on fertile ground.

In fact Cesare Mori is blowing smoke out his nostrils, so enraged is he when he learns that not only were the Saccos able to slip away, but the townsfolk of Raffadali had a great time of it, thumbing their noses at the special forces.

And so, arriving at the easy (and correct) conclusion that the Sacco brothers could not remain for very long at large without the help of the local population, Mori decides, in his typical fashion, to set an example that will discourage, once and for all, anyone wishing to lend aid or support to the fugitives.

There's one problem, however, the same as there's been all along: Before fighting the Saccos, one must define what they are. Until proven otherwise, the Saccos have never been mafiosi; indeed they ended up becoming fugitives precisely because they had opposed the Mafia.

Therefore, Cesare Mori, at least in theory, should consider them his allies, not his enemies.

Then why go up against them?

Because, according to what people say, they've allegedly killed at least two Mafia bosses. They are therefore murderers, even if they have cleansed the town of people who had dozens of murders on their consciences.

But, even admitting that it was indeed the Saccos who killed the two Mafia bosses—though some reasonable doubt is legitimate, since not a shred of evidence has ever been found— what need was there to send the special forces and all their rig- marole to arrest them?

The matter of the arrest could very well have been left to regular law enforcement, which certainly, sooner or later, would have nabbed the Sacco brothers.

Finally: How much did this dogged Sacco hunt really have to do with the task Mussolini had assigned the prefect?

Mori, at this point, recalls that his mandate also includes the fight against banditry. Even though at the time, in all of Sicily, there must have been at best only two or three bandits left, and in bad shape at that.

Still, that was the solution.

To turn the Sacco brothers into bandits.

And bandits, ever since the beginning of time, are part of a band—a gang, in other words.

And, just like that, the "notorious Sacco gang" is born.

But can one really tell the press that the gang is charged with killing mafiosi guilty of multiple murders?

No, one can't. Because the people are then liable to sympa- thize with them.

Thus Mori, every time he talks to journalists, never forgets to remind them of how dangerous the Sacco gang is, given as they are to looting, holdups, burglary, and stealing livestock.

And, as an example, he cites a collection made in town to help them—except that in his version, the voluntary collection becomes an ongoing extortion racket.

Only the people of Raffadali themselves can attest that Mori is making it all up, but the majority of them are unable to read or write; and so, little by little, Sicilians end up believing the calumny, also because with each passing day the newspapers keep featuring bold headlines about the misdeeds of the "notorious Sacco gang."

When Mori becomes convinced he's properly softened up public opinion, he moves into action.

An action convenient to him and to Commendatore V.

*

On May 3, 1926, the town of Raffadali awakes to find itself entirely surrounded by special forces.

No one can leave town. All the peasants on their way to work in their fields in the countryside are sent back home.

At a certain point other special forces units burst into town and begin arresting people.

Tommaso Cuffaro, former Socialist mayor; Francesco Gueli, former Socialist Vice Mayor; Salvatore Motta, former Socialist councilor; Baldassare Gueli, notary, along with his five brothers-in-law; Salvatore Gueli, postmaster; and Alfonso Motta, local medical officer, are all placed under arrest for the charge of having given aid and shelter to the "notorious Sacco gang."

Another hundred or so people—including municipal clerks, shop owners, landowners, and peasants—are handcuffed and brought in under the same charge.

But the arrest that sparks the most clamor is that of the ex-mayor, Commendator Alfonso Di Benedetto, who is accused outright of complicity with the Saccos in the murder of Cuffaro the overseer.

Later, but still the same morning, the special forces also put the cuffs on the Sacco brothers' mother, who is well over seventy years old; Vanni's wife; Vincenzo's wife; the Saccos' mother's sister, Zà Grazia, eighty years old, over the power-of-attorney business; and the two Mangione brothers, first cousins of the Saccos.

Mori's men, moreover, do not leave a single house in Raffadali unsearched.

They tear open pillows and mattresses, kick down closed doors, throw some furniture out into the streets.

More than a police operation, it looks like a raid by brigands.

It was Mori who wanted his men to act this way, brutally, angrily, to frighten everyone.

But since they make no distinction between criminals and law-abiding citizens and treat everyone the same way, the end result is that even the honest folks who at first warmly welcomed the news that someone was coming to fight the Mafia, now change their minds, after being subjected to such behavior.

Meanwhile the Saccos' elderly mother is interrogated without interruption for an entire day and night without being given anything to eat or drink. They want her to tell them where her sons are, and overwhelm her with questions.

The woman doesn't know where they are. She really doesn't, and is therefore unable to answer.

So at this point all of the Saccos' women—their mother, the mother's sister, and the brothers' wives—are taken to Girgenti Prison.

Mori spreads the word that they will not be released until the Saccos turn themselves in of their own accord.

The repressive measure, however, achieves no concrete results.

And so, the cousins Mangione, after fifteen days in custody, are presented with an ultimatum: either they write a declaration saying that Vanni and Alfonso Sacco have revealed to them all the details concerning the murder of the mafioso over-seer Giovanni Terrazzino, or they will be charged with criminal collusion and locked up.

The two refuse to sign the declaration.

As a result, they are sent from the prison back to the Carabinieri compound, where they are subjected to harsh tortures that leave marks on their bodies so severe that the consequences thereof are later confirmed by expert medical examiners.

After a week of such treatment, their resistance erodes, and they sign the statement.

With the swiftest of trials, Mori succeeds in obtaining a few convictions for accessory after the fact: 86 of the more than 100 people arrested are sentenced to anywhere from four to nine years in prison; Mamma Sacco gets eight years, her sister likewise.

For the trick they pulled by escaping from the special forces, Alfonso and Vanni are sentenced in absentia to twelve years.

At the trial of appeal, the aunt will be acquitted, the mother's sentence halved.

The cousins Mangione's false declaration will be used to reopen the trial for the murder of the mafioso Giovanni Terrazzino, a crime for which Vanni and Alfonso have already been acquitted once.

*

One day when the Saccos, in despair, no longer know which way to turn, one person manages to approach them, a peasant who works on the lands belonging to Commendatore V.

"The commendatore told me to tell you that now is the right time to turn yourselves in."

But the Saccos know it's a ruse.

They realized it when they learned who the persons were that Mori had arrested—not common criminals or mafiosi, but socialists and personal enemies of the commendatore.

Apparently the commendatore used the Saccos' flight from justice to give Mori a reason for the arrests.

And, in fact, with the field now cleared of his political opponents, Commendatore V is almost immediately elected mayor of Raffadali.

The Saccos no longer feel like turning themselves in.

XIII
CAPTURE

Now that Cesare Mori has shown himself to be a man capable of anything, to be the first to pay no mind whatsoever to the rule of law, people start thinking twice before lending a hand to the Saccos.

The mafiosi themselves, just to avoid jail time, wouldn't hesitate for a minute to turn them in to the special forces if they happened to learn where the fugitives were hiding.

And so the Saccos are forced to keep continually on the move, from the woods to the mountains, from one town to the next, one cave to another, feeling more and more weary, with the special forces always breathing hard down their necks.

On the evening of Friday, October 15, 1926, dead tired from running and lack of sleep, they find temporary shelter in a cottage, a white cube some four meters square on the Mizzaro domain, near the town of Sant'Angelo Muxaro.

They are almost out of provisions.

"I'm going into town to see if any grocers are still open and buy some stuff to eat," says Alfonso.

But Vanni stops him.

"No. Better not. We're outsiders here. A new face might arouse suspicion."

In a haversack, they have a loaf of hard bread, half a round of cheese, and a flask still full of wine.

They share what little is left, then draw lots to determine who must stand guard until dawn. It falls to Alfonso.

As Alfonso heads outside, Vanni and Salvatore go and lie down with Marzullo and La Porta to get some sleep.

The night passes peacefully, so much so that at a certain point Alfonso falls into a light sleep.

But then he's suddenly awakened by the furious barking of dogs that until that moment had been perfectly quiet.

He opens his eyes, sees the dawn's first light.

But why are the dogs still barking?

Could someone be approaching?

Alfonso starts to worry. By now he has the instincts of a hunted animal, and so he climbs up a tree to look farther into the distance.

Since he also has binoculars, he clearly sees, far up on the main road, some stationary, empty military trucks.

If those trucks are empty—Alfonso reasons correctly—it means the soldiers they were transporting are already in the area.

They haven't got a minute to lose.

Surely someone saw them enter the cottage the previous evening, recognized them, and went and snitched on them.

He jumps hastily down from the tree, goes into the cottage, and starts waking up the four men, who are sleeping deeply.

But they all freeze when they hear a voice outside, but very near, shout:

"You're surrounded! Give yourselves up!"

Everyone's on their feet now, fully awake, loaded guns in hand.

But they realize that there's little or nothing they can do this time. They have to admit to themselves that they've let themselves get caught by surprise, like a bunch of beginners.

They don't even have time to exchange half a word before the besiegers open fire without warning on the cottage, in a hellish fusillade.

But how many of them are firing out there? A hundred? Nobody returns the special forces' fire.

Vanni and Alfonso, lying belly-down on the floor, feverishly consult each other, speaking more with their eyes than with their mouths.

They've come to the end.

Before them lies the invisible borderline which, in their minds, marks the passage into illegality.

The only possible escape, surrounded as they are, is to come out all five at once, shooting blindly in all directions, come what may, and attempt to open a breach.

But shooting at the forces of order means declaring oneself outside the law, and they're not outlaws. They especially don't feel like outlaws.

They are, in short, in the exact situation Sergeant Jannuzzo had lucidly foreseen.

"Save your own lives and surrender!" shouts the same voice as before.

Vanni then looks at each of his comrades one by one, and each of his comrades, one by one, nods "yes."

The only choice left to them is to obey the order.

But they don't manage in time.

The shooting resumes and lasts five eternal minutes.

Then it ends, and the same voice as before commands:

"Throw your weapons outside the door!"

The five men look at each other. Vanni gestures to Alfonso.

Alfonso cautiously opens the door only as much as necessary, and throws out, as far as possible from the house, almost with anger, the weapons his mates pass to him.

"Are you unarmed? Throw out your knives as well."

They'd forgotten about the knives. They throw these out too.

"Do you have any other weapons?"

"No," Vanni answers.

"Come out one by one with your hands in the air!"

Who should go out first? The five men have a moment of hesitation. Then Vanni starts to head for the door.

"No, I'll go out first," says La Porta, stopping him. "I haven't done anything wrong, after all."

And he goes out, hands raised.

"Stop right there!"

La Porta stops barely two steps away from the cottage, as Alfonso is coming out.

"Stop right there and stand beside your comrade!"

Before them is a row of special forces troops, one knee to the ground, rifles pointed.

Quickly all five men are lined up, shoulder to shoulder, in front of the cottage, their hands in the air.

"Is there anyone else still inside?"

"No, nobody," replies Vanni.

For thirty seconds the scene freezes: five men in a row, and some ten soldiers with rifles aimed. All around them, a sea of soldiers stare on in silence.

Nobody speaks. The dogs keep on barking.

"Why aren't they coming to handcuff us?" Vanni asks himself in bewilderment.

Then, all of a sudden, the unbelievable happens.

The kneeling soldiers open fire all at once, like an execution squad.

Pietro La Porta is struck in the heart and falls to the ground.

Alfonso collapses, gravely wounded in the head, then more rifle shots hit him in the forearm and the left leg.

Salvatore takes a bullet through the chest.

Vanni and Marzullo are only grazed by the shots and sustain no injuries. But they remain as still as statues, frozen in horror and disdain for such cowardly treachery.

But it's not over yet.

Mouths drooling with rage, the soldiers who'd been standing by, watching, now let fly at the corpse, the wounded, and the two still unharmed men, unleashing a savage, animal fury amid shouts, curses, and insults.

They start kicking Pietro La Porta's lifeless body in the face with their hobnailed boots, rendering him almost unrecognizable.

Salvatore, half-unconscious from his wound, has his stomach run through with a bayonet.

They break Alfonso's wounded arm with the butts of their rifles.

Vanni and Marzullo, knocked down to the ground under a hail of blows to the legs from the soldiers' rifle butts, and buried in kicks, punches, and bayonet thrusts, are quickly little more than blood-drenched dummies.

It's a proper lynching.

The unit's commander, Lieutenant Nuvoletti, arrives at a gallop and, shouting orders, manages to end the butchery.

But at the same time Nuvoletti is worried about providing his men with an alibi for what they've done.

This he does by having the weapons the Saccos surrendered fired repeatedly into the air.

That way he can claim that the killing as well as the injuries was the result of a firefight.

But he makes an egregious mistake. He neglects to have them fire the Mauser, the most powerful and deadly weapon in the Saccos' arsenal, and Vanni's personal gun.

At the trial it will come out that in fact the weapon, though in perfect functioning order, was definitely not used in the sham shoot-out.

Nuvoletti is a careful man, and so he has the shells of the cartridges he had his men fire with the Saccos' guns collected and set aside.

He's perfectly aware that he will have to prove, in every way, that there was a firefight, otherwise how will he explain the death and the ravaged bodies of the other four?

To be completely safe, he even has the cottage burnt down.

All the while the injured lie on the ground, moaning and losing blood, and no one comes to their aid.

*

At last the dead and injured are loaded roughly onto an uncovered truck and conveyed, under the escort of the special forces that took part in the operation, to Raffadali.

The whole town must be made to see that the "notorious Sacco gang" has been annihilated.

The people of Raffadali are waiting for them, having already heard the news from a few peasants who had raced into town on horseback to inform them.

The whole thing looks, in every way, like a scene from a Western.

As the procession passes along the main street of Raffadali at a walking pace, flanked by utterly silent crowds, the bells of the Mother Church begin to toll the knell.

It's the parish priest himself who gave the order.

"Why are the bells ringing?" asks Lieutenant Nuvoletti.

"Because there's been a death," replies the priest.

Yet everyone knows perfectly well what the priest's intention was in ordering the sacristan to toll the knell: not to commemorate poor Pietro La Porta, but to say goodbye to the hope that the Saccos had awakened in the townsfolk by liberating them, for a short while, from Mafia oppression.

Suddenly a little boy breaks away from the silent crowd and runs up and spits with scorn at the cart carrying the Saccos.

"Don't do anything to that boy! Don't touch him!" Vanni shouts with the little breath he has left.

He doesn't want his friends to get angry with the boy and start hitting him. He is genuinely tired of violence.

Alfonso, though wounded and utterly drained of strength, is leaning on one elbow and casting glances left and right. At last his gaze encounters what it was so desperately looking for: the eyes of the girl he loves. They are filled with tears.

He'll see those eyes again one day, almost forty years later.

*

There is still one sordid sequel to the animal rage of the special forces.

In the courtyard of the Carabinieri compound, Captain Tomei, the commander of that particular unit, awaits the arrival of the procession.

Vanni is helping Alfonso get down from the cart.

At that moment the captain, who is on horseback, spurs his mount and charges the two men as if to knock them over, yelling like a madman.

"I'll kill you myself, you criminals!"

In a flash, Lieutenant Nuvoletti rushes over and shunts them aside with a powerful thrust.

Already very unsteady on their feet, the two men fall to the ground.

Nuvoletti helps them up and personally escorts them to safety inside the compound, turning them over to the local carabinieri.

For the entire time of their internment at the compound, these local officers, knowing the truth of the matter, treat them humanely. They summon some doctors to treat their wounds and make sure they want for nothing.

Just a few days later, however, is the 28th of October, the anniversary of the Fascist March on Rome, now a national holiday.

A hundred or so Fascists, from Raffadali and the nearby towns, surround the compound. Among their number, wearing Fascist black shirts, are also a few powerful mafiosi who have skillfully trimmed their sails to catch the prevailing winds.

"Give us the Saccos! We'll show them what justice is!"

They want to lynch them, and are armed with billy clubs and daggers.

The marshal comes out with four officers and invites the Fascists to dissolve the assembly.

But the crowd grows even more enraged.

"Give them to us or we'll come and get them!"

The marshal then raises his arm and the four officers fire. In the air.

The Fascists run away.

That evening, just to be safe, the Saccos are taken to Girgenti Prison.

On the way there, Salvatore's and Alfonso's wounds reopen.

XIV
Taking Stock

Owing to the great zeal of Prefect Cesare Mori's agents, all the killings that occurred during our time as fugitives were placed on our, the Sacco brothers', account. The authorities did not take into consideration the torrent of criminality that had rained down on the people of Raffadali during the First World War and immediately thereafter. The people had every right to take revenge and vent their resentment against these criminals, especially knowing that it was the Sacco brothers who were taking it all on their shoulders—that is, taking on all the charges for all the crimes committed. And so, Prefect Mori got to work setting up three trials: one for four homicides attributed to us, Giovanni and Alfonso Sacco; two for homicides charged to Salvatore Sacco; and one for a murder charged to the late Filippo Marzullo, who lost his life during the terrible Second World War, from an illness caused by malnutrition."

So writes Alfonso.

Just to put things in order, then, let's see how many homicides the Saccos were accused of committing while they were fugitives.

There were seven in all.

A few murder charges were lost along the way, when it was shown, beyond a reasonable doubt, that the Saccos had nothing to do with them. A few of the accusations of which the Saccos had been acquitted at earlier trials were, however, expressly revived, so that the brothers would appear before the judge with serious charges hanging over them.

However—and this is an important point to remember—at the moment of their arrest, there was only one charge in effect against them: the murder of Terrazzino. More precisely, they had in fact been previously acquitted of the charge, but the courts had appealed.[6]

Then, while they were in jail, charges were brought for the killings of Cuffaro, Plano, and Mangione.

As for La Porta, the authorities figured it was best not to charge him with anything, since they'd shot him dead as he was surrendering.

*

They begin with the killing of Cuffaro.

In a "brilliant" operation (though it's unclear why they waited three years to conduct it), the Carabinieri arrest two peasants, the D'Anna cousins.

They are both good men, with clean records and never any run-ins whatsoever with the law. They work on the lands belonging to Commendator Alfonso Di Benedetto, who was four times mayor and was in jail during the incursion of Mori's special forces.

The two unlucky cousins are subjected to out-and-out torture for fifteen days, to the point that one ends up with a hernia, while the other nearly loses sight in one eye.

But the courts get what they want in the end.

The D'Anna cousins are so battered at this point that they would admit to anything. More precisely: they'll say whatever their torturers want them to say.

---

[6] Italian law has no "double jeopardy" provision, a fact that made it even easier for the Fascist regime to bend the legal system to its whims. (t.n.)

(Let us not forget Manzoni's *Story of the Infamous Column*, where Mora, unable to stand any more torture, says to the judge: "Look, I'll say what you want me to say.")

"Where were the two of you in the moments before Cuffaro was killed?"

"We'd gone to the country house of Commendatore Di Benedetto."

"What did you go there for?"

"We were supposed to talk about farming stuff."

"Was the commendatore alone?"

"No, he had Vanni and Alfonso Sacco with him."

"What happened?"

"As we was talkin', Vanni Sacco tol' me to go an' see if Cuffaro was on his way back from the Baron's."

"So to return to his home in Raffadali, Cuffaro necessarily had to go past Di Benedetto's house?"

"Yessir."

"And did you go and look?"

"Yessir. But first I ast Vanni why he wanted to know."

"And what did he say?"

"He said he wanted to kill Cuffaro."

"And then what?"

"Well, seein' that we was undecided, the commendatore said to us: 'Didn't you hear what Vanni said to you? Go and do it.' An' so we done it."

"What did you do?"

"As soon as we saw Cuffaro comin', we tol' the Saccos, and they come runnin' out, took up position, an', soon as Cuffaro was in range, they shot him."

"Did you see or hear anything else?"

"Yessir. After the shots, the commendatore went to have a look. An' then Cuffaro, who was still hangin' on, soon as he saw him, ast him to help him."

"And what did Di Benedetto do?"

"He started laughin'. Then he said: 'How can I help you? Can't you see you're dead?' An' then he came back inside."

This scene rings so fantastical that Alfonso comments:

"It would take the pen of a Victor Hugo or another great writer to express the full deluge that would spring from Cuffaro's words to Di Benedetto and from the latter's statement."

A literary deluge, that is.

At the 1923 trial, the one that acquitted the Saccos, the autopsy clearly demonstrated that the single shot that killed the Mafia boss hit him right in the middle of the forehead and allowed him no time to make so much as a peep.

When later called before the judge, however, the D'Anna cousins retract everything, accuse the Carabinieri of having tortured them, and present expert medical reports attesting to the torments to which they'd been subjected.

Conclusion: Di Benedetto and the D'Annas are released.

But the killing of Cuffaro remains on the Sacco brothers' shoulders.

*

The killing of the Saccos' cousins, Plano and Mangione, resulted, as we've already said, from a sort of misunderstanding.

Let's have Alfonso tell us firsthand how things went, since it's a rather important question:

"On the 9th of September two of our second cousins were killed: Giovanni Plano and Stefano Mangione. Following the investigation and the interrogations conducted by Sergeant Montalbano as well as the investigating magistrate, the authorities ruled out armed robbery and murder, because whoever did the killing intended neither to kill them nor to rob them. They came to this conclusion based on where our relatives were at that moment. On their way back from selling some animals at the Ribera fair, Plano and Mangione had been sitting at that drinking trough, eating and resting, for a good while, unmolested. As they were setting off again, however, Mangione's young son noticed there were some people behind the rocks, gesturing to him to keep on going; but the boy went back and informed the others of this, and his uncle Vincenzo, who was armed with a rifle, thinking they wanted to rob him, started shooting, triggering a firefight that ended in the deaths of those two good men, who for all their lives had never done anything but toil honestly to feed their families! This is what our cousin, Vincenzo Mangione, told my brother Giovanni and me after the painful event, which occurred in the company of his brothers, including Francesco, our sister Filomena's husband. The person really responsible—the cause, that is, of the deaths of those two dear relatives of ours—can be said to be our own cousin, Vincenzo Mangione."

Thus, from this account, taken from the *Memorial* Alfonso wrote after his release from prison, it emerges that there were three Mangione brothers present at the firefight: Stefano (who lost his life in it, along with Plano), Vincenzo (who first started firing), and Francesco (the husband of the Saccos' sister); that Vincenzo Mangione started firing for fear that the men positioned behind the rocks wanted to rob them; and that the men behind the rocks reacted to the gunfire by killing Giovanni Plano and Stefano Mangione.

But who were these mysterious men behind the rocks?

Why were they there?

Who were they waiting for?

Certainly not the Mangiones, since they'd signaled to the boy to keep on going, to walk on, to get out of the way—as though, in short, his group of people constituted a hindrance.

In his *Memorial*, Alfonso never gives the names of the men hiding behind the rocks. Apparently he did not know who they were.

However, in his *Biography of the "Notorious Sacco Gang,"* which he wrote and published in 1959, when still in prison at Saluzzo, Alfonso told a slightly different story.

"On the 9th of September 1924, when returning from the fair at Ribera, Stefano Mangione, our cousin and the brother of our sister's husband, and Giovanni Plano, husband of a cousin of ours, were killed at a drinking trough. They were both fathers, both honest farmers, both fine, upright men! They were killed when one of the Mangione brothers (Vincenzo), after seeing some malfeasants lying in ambush, started firing his rifle at them for fear of being robbed, triggering a firefight that led to the death of those two fathers. [. . .] Returning from the same fair were a group of mafiosi that included two big bosses: Francesco Giglione, and Salvatore Terrazzino, the butcher. Informed of the incident by a sentry of theirs, they headed out to the country, but took another route and eventually made it back into town. In order to have these further crimes blamed on us, these mafiosi spread the rumor that the malfeasants were lying in wait not for the Mangione brothers, but for them, and therefore it could only have been the Sacco brothers."

Here, too, Alfonso neglects to name the men lying in wait.

But he does name the two mafiosi, one of whose brother, Giovanni Terrazzino, having taken command after Salvatore ended up in prison, would later be shot, with people believing, beyond any doubt, that it was the Saccos who'd done it.

But if the story of the boy seeing masked men behind the rocks, and the men signaling him to keep on going, is true, then this means that the group lying in ambush were not waiting for the first group, the one with the Mangiones, but the second one, with the two Mafia bosses.

*

Years later, Alfonso, now 87, is interviewed by a journalist by the name of Giuseppe Pirrello.

Here is his account of this killing, as related by the journalist:

"It was the day of the annual livestock fair at Cattolica, and everyone was going there to do some kind of business or other. Even the overseers went. Around sunset, as everyone was heading home, the overseers started worrying about a possible ambush by the Sacco brothers. And so they told our two cousins, whose name was Mangione, to walk a few hundred yards ahead of them and tell them if they noticed anything unusual. When the Mangiones got to the well at 'Da li ciciri,' they saw some suspicious faces. They started running back towards the overseers, but the Saccos started shooting, and the two cousins were killed."

This makes no sense whatsoever, with respect to the first and second accounts of the event.

Now it's two of the three Mangiones who walk on ahead, but no longer the boy.

And the overseers who'd figured in the *Biography* reappear in the group.

The men behind the rocks are now the Saccos.

And it's the Saccos who shoot first.

These are very grave admissions.

Why didn't the two Mangiones recognize their cousins, the Saccos?

Apparently because the Saccos had covered their faces with shawls.

And it's possible they were behind the rocks with their faces covered because they were waiting for the overseers to pass in order to shoot them—though there is no mention whatsoever of them in the *Memorial*.

But there surely had to have been some kind of mistake, since the Saccos would never have fired first against a brother-in-law and cousin.

The point of it all is that Alfonso is acknowledging the fact that it was they who killed the two unlucky cousins caught between the overseers and the Saccos.

And this raises a great many doubts about what actually happened, apart from the double murder at the drinking trough.

*

So, to conclude, four murders are placed on the Saccos' account: those of Cuffaro, Terrazzino, Plano, and Mangione.

And then there's the firefight before the Saccos' capture.

And the collection labeled an ongoing extortion.

Then the escape from the first attempted arrest.

Then there was the conviction in the first instance, but just for Vanni, for that fake theft of livestock, which Vanni appealed.

And there should also be the prison escape, but nobody's talking about that.

XV
THE TRIAL

The Saccos' trial begins in late March 1928.

Vanni, Alfonso, and Salvatore are charged with two counts of murder, Vincenzo and Girolamo with "aggravated criminal association."

Inside the prison the five men are not only handcuffed, but chained one to the other in such a way that they can't even move. Loaded then onto a covered truck along with some ten armed carabinieri, they come out of the prison.

But right outside the main entrance they find two rows of carabinieri for the truck to pass between. The double row of carabinieri continues uninterrupted all the way to the main entrance to the courthouse.

That's almost two kilometers' worth of carabinieri, to form a protective cordon.

Never had anyone seen such a display of force.

The whole thing was staged to underscore just how dangerous "the notorious Sacco gang" really was, and to foreground the triumph of Prefect Mori and his men.

The defendants plead not guilty.

The first thing the presiding judge wants to know is what happened during the firefight that led to the capture of the Sacco brothers, and so he calls Lieutenant Giovanni Nuvoletti to testify.

The lieutenant says that once they'd surrounded the cottage, he ordered the Saccos to surrender and began to approach the door, when he was shot at twice, the bullets whistling past his head.

"Where did these shots come from?"

"From the half-closed door."

Since the judge wants to be certain it was the Saccos who fired first, he calls Sergeant Dascoli to the stand.

"Did the Saccos shoot first?"

"Yes, sir."

"From where?"

"From the roof of the cottage."

"Are you sure? The lieutenant says they fired from the door."

"No, sir, the door was closed. They fired from the roof."

The presiding judge attempts to reconcile the contradiction between the two testimonies.

"Maybe the shots came diagonally, and so you merely thought they came from the roof."

"No, your honor, I actually saw the tiles flying in the air!"

At this point, everyone becomes utterly confused.

Because if the tiles were flying in the air, it means that the shots were fired *at* the roof, not *from* the roof.

Therefore, if the Saccos ever even did fire, they fired in the air. Then how was it that the lieutenant heard the bullets whistling past his head?

At this point the presiding judge, seeing that the situation could take a dangerous turn, calls Nuvoletti back to the stand, but asks him no further questions as to who fired first.

"How long did the firefight last?"

"Two hours, without interruption."

"Do you have any idea how many shots were fired on both sides?"

"I had all the shells collected."

"And how many are there?"

"Eighty."

Everyone is taken aback.

What? Only eighty shots fired in a firefight that lasted two hours? Isn't that a rather small amount?

"How much ammunition did the Saccos have?"

"A great deal. If we hadn't broken into the house, they could have held out for hours longer."

"And how many of you were there in the special forces?"

"More than two hundred."

"Why did the Saccos never use the Mauser?"

"I can't answer that question."

At this point the public prosecutor, seeing the question of the firefight on shaky ground, stands up.

"I would point out," he says, "that if we disprove the firefight, we end one game and we begin a new one!"

These words are uttered in a threatening tone that means nothing and everything.

The prosecutor goes on to explain to the court that a firefight was ideologically inevitable in as much as the Saccos, given the political ideals they embraced, were subversives who hated the forces of order.

And he said he was sorry that Paolo Tuttolomondo wasn't also behind bars.

"And who's that?" asks the presiding judge, who has never seen that name mentioned in the trial documents.

"He's the Saccos' cousin! Their political inspiration, who unfortunately has escaped to America! Tuttolomondo is a passionate follower of the Bolshevik Antonio Gramsci!"

The defense asks how it could be that, in a firefight lasting two hours, there were one death and two grave injuries on the Saccos' side, whereas not a single man among the special forces sustained even the slightest wound, despite the deadly aim of Vanni Sacco?

And so everyone becomes convinced that the famous firefight never happened.

And, as a result, the charge is changed to simply "resisting arrest."

But if they were only resisting arrest, how did someone actually get killed?

For now, however, it's best to drop the whole thing, and to go no further down that path.

The Saccos are sentenced to a mere two years.

*

They then move on to the murder of Cuffaro, the Mafia boss.

Since the D'Annas have retracted their confession, there is only one remaining witness, Vincenzo Galvano, eighty years of age, in rather poor health and almost totally blind, to the point that he has to be carried bodily to the witness stand.

Galvano says he was unable to recognize the two who fired the shots because they were too far away, and he didn't see very well because of his trachomatous conjunctivitis.

The prosecutor bolts to his feet and starts speaking in dialect, threatening the old man:

"Zù Vicè, yer gonna spend the night tonight at Santo Vito prison!"

Santo Vito is the official name of Girgenti Prison.

But the old man stands firm in his declaration.

The judge intervenes:

"Are you reneging? You told the Carabinieri you recognized Giovanni and Alfonso Sacco, and then you reconfirmed it to the investigating magistrate!"

"Yessir, tha'ss wha' they made me say now, but when I was quessioned the first time, I told the truth."

"You were questioned earlier?"

"Yessir, I was, in 1923, an' I said azackly what I'm sayin' now."

The prosecutor stands up, claiming Galvano is trying to reshuffle the deck, and that he was never questioned in 1923.

The judge picks up a sheet of paper and says:

"Galvano, it's written here that 'when asked, the subject

reports never having been questioned earlier in connection with this trial.' Why didn't you tell us you'd already been interrogated?"

"'Cause tha's what they tol' me to say."

The defense digs in its heels and demands to see all the minutes of the 1923 trial. And it succeeds in overcoming the protests of the prosecution.

At this point the defense, waiving its own right to an expert opinion, asks the court to arrange a medical examination to establish to what degree Galvano could actually see five years earlier, given the current grave condition of his eyes.

The presiding judge holds a hearing in camera and then rejects the request.

The Saccos are given life sentences on the basis of Galvano's second testimony, the one clearly extracted from him by force.

*

Midway through the trial, something curious happened.

The public prosecutor, in the course of his harangue, brought to the court's attention that the trial could not be allowed to end with everyone kissing and making up.

Among other reasons given, he said that the hunt and capture of the Saccos had cost the state nine million lire.

At this point the Saccos realized they were finished.

With nine million—writes Alfonso—you could, in those days, build an entire city. A shocking, impossible figure!

Only a conviction, in the end, could justify such a waste, such a drain on the public purse. *That* was why they'd had them escorted through two kilometers of carabinieri! *That* was why Lieutenant Nuvoletti said that there were two hundred men in his contingent of special forces, when the Saccos saw barely a hundred!

As of that moment, and until the end of the trial, the Saccos refused to return to the courtroom.

*

The trial for the killing of Terrazzino was even worse.

In the courtroom the written testimony of the Galvano boy was read aloud.

The lad himself didn't come in person because he'd been sent to America, in case he decided to change his mind.

And on the basis of that single testimony, the three Saccos each got another life sentence.

*

For the killing of Plano and Mangione, they couldn't find a single witness for the prosecution. The Saccos were convicted solely on the basis of the results of the Carabinieri's own investigation.

*

The verdict also specified that the Saccos must spend the first twelve years of their life sentences in "silent segregation"—that is, in solitary confinement, in a single cell, without being allowed to speak to the prison guards, and with no right to one hour a day in the open air.

*

Vincenzo was sentenced to ten years for aggravated criminal association, and to another twelve for having organized a collection in town for those innocent parties who'd been unjustly imprisoned, the same collection that had been labeled "ongoing extortion."

*

Girolamo got four years for simple criminal association.

*

While Vanni was already serving his life sentence, the trial that had begun seven years earlier, the one in which he'd been found guilty of armed animal theft, the one that had started everything, finally, between appeals and repeals, reached its ultimate conclusion.

On October 12, 1929, Vanni was fully acquitted on all counts.

Nobody said a word about the prison escape, because there was no mention of it in the trial documents.

PRISON AND PARDON

Salvatore, Vanni, and Alfonso begin to make the hellish rounds of Italy's prisons and penitentiaries: Agrigento, Palermo, Noto, Portici, Poggioreale, Campobasso, Portolongone, Ventotene, Turi, Saluzzo.

*

They meet some important people.

"At Ventotene," writes Alfonso, "they allowed me to read, at first. I met many victims of Fascist persecution and was able to study and gain a better grasp of the social and political situation of the age. I met Umberto Terracini, who was also in jail at the time. Then, by order of the Fascists, the prison authorities took my books away. I couldn't read, but I could still think. My family was socialist, and we have remained socialist. Indeed, our ideas grew stronger in prison. Vanni and Girolamo managed to end up in the same prison as Antonio Gramsci."

*

At Turi Prison, Gramsci nourishes a certain sympathy for the two Sacco brothers. Who in turn are literally overwhelmed by the man's learning and humanity.

At the same prison there's a poor wretch of limited intelligence who bears a striking resemblance to Gramsci: the same body type, the same physical deformities. Kidding around with

Gramsci one day, Vanni suggests a plan of escape from the prison based on his strong resemblance to the other inmate. They often laugh about it.

When Girolamo, having served his sentence, is later released, Gramsci gives him some papers to take out of the prison.

*

Girolamo returns to Raffadali, gets married, and eventually has six children.

Immediately after the fall of Fascism, he devotes himself heart and soul to obtaining a pardon for his three brothers. He becomes friends with the Christian Democratic politicians of the time, who promise to help him in exchange for votes.

But all his requests are routinely rejected.

And to think that in 1960, Girolamo managed to get no less than 5000 signatures supporting a pardon.

Which means that, since Raffadali had 12,294 inhabitants at the time, everyone had signed except for the children, the illiterates, and the emigrants.

Salvatore, Vanni, and Alfonso don't want to be pardoned, however, and indeed they do not support Girolamo's efforts.

They want a retrial.

According to Alfonso, the spokesman for the three, the trial was unfairly conducted and vitiated by an a priori will to convict. The judges, in short, surrendered to Fascist pressures and came up with the three life sentences out of pure and simple political obedience.

*

None other than the chief prosecutor of Saluzzo, in his capacity as prison warden, requests a pardon on his own initiative, in view of the Saccos' exemplary conduct.

But the fact that the three brothers will not countersign the initiative dooms it to failure.

*

In the meantime Salvatore Di Benedetto, son of the former mayor of Raffadali, after a long sojourn in Milan as an organizer for the clandestine Italian Communist Party—which brought him into close contact with intellectuals such as Vittorini, Treccani, and Steiner—and then a valorous stint as a partisan fighter, becomes mayor in turn and is later elected senator.

He suggests that Vanni write a letter to his fellow senator, Umberto Terracini, asking him to take an interest, as a lawyer, in their case. And in the meantime he tells Terracini the story of the Sacco brothers.

Terracini replies to Vanni in a letter dated February 15, 1962.

He states that he has been "deeply affected" by the whole story, adding that "the fate that has struck your family is indeed tragic, leading as it has to a harsh, ruthless life sentence for three brothers at once." He goes on: "I think it may be the only case of its kind in the history of Italian justice, which yet has known a great many other iniquitous episodes."

He concludes by saying that he is willing to try to set things right.

*

And so Alfonso writes to him, giving him all the necessary information for locating the trial minutes, and tells him that the Saccos want a retrial.

Terracini's reply is immediate, and specific.

It would take a long time to be granted a retrial, and they need to take into consideration that Salvatore and Vanni are by now well advanced in years. Wouldn't it be better, Terracini asks, to gain a pardon first, and then immediately begin procedures for retrial?

Alfonso accepts his suggestion. And Terracini gets down to work. For free.

*

The Saccos, in any case, have been reduced to poverty.

They had to sell everything to pay the lawyers and support themselves during their time as fugitives. In more recent times, they've managed to survive on collections made by the citizens of Raffadali.

*

In October of 1962, the warden of Saluzzo Prison summons Alfonso in total secrecy and informs him that the President of the Republic, Antonio Segni, has approved and signed the pardon, thanks to the intelligent efforts of Terracini.

But there's one condition: if the three Saccos, once set free, decide to settle on the Italian mainland, they can all be released together, at once; if they plan instead to settle in Sicily, they can only come out one at a time, at six-month intervals.

*

But the Saccos have no family living on the mainland who might house and feed them. The one who decides the order of their release is Alfonso, who demands that the warden keep the matter secret. He must never tell his brothers that the decision was his.

*

On October 12, 1962, Salvatore is the first to be released. He is seventy-four years old and very sick.

On April 12, 1963, Vanni comes out.

On October 30 of the same year, Alfonso, the last one remaining in prison, receives a telegram from Terracini, informing him that the order for his release has arrived.

*

Once back in Raffadali, Alfonso marries Pina Crapanzano

She was the girl he last saw in 1926, when making his way through the parted crowd, wounded and handcuffed.

Pina waited for him for nearly forty years, never once losing hope.

The Mafia not only robbed Alfonso and Pina of forty years of life together, but also denied them the possibility of having children.

*

Vanni for his part already had two children, Luigi and Antonina, before the Mafia ruined his life. After his release, he obtains a passport and moves to California with his wife, to live in the home of his daughter, Antonina, where he remains until the end of his days.

*

His other child, young Luigi, died while his father was in prison. Mysteriously.

Taken to Pompeii, to a boarding school for the children of parents serving life sentences, he dies in circumstances that have forever remained obscure, along with another boy, the son of the same Marzullo who accompanied the Saccos in many of their adventures and misadventures and was arrested and convicted along with them.

Isn't it a strange coincidence that the sons of two men who fought the Mafia together should die together, at the same time?

The circumstances of the two boys' deaths were never revealed to the parents.

Some have surmised, perhaps not incorrectly, that the long arm of the Mafia reached all the way to Pompeii to complete their atrocious vendetta, through the liquidation of two innocent boys.

*

Sometimes history likes to play tricks. In 1943, shortly after the Allies landed in Sicily and restored power and honor to the Mafia,[7] alongside such names as Vizzini and Genco Russo, now back in the limelight, we also find that of Vanni Sacco.

But it's just a case of two different people with the same name. This new Vanni Sacco isn't even related to our Vanni, and he's not from Raffadali.

In the future, however, people will begin to confuse the two with increasing frequency.

---

[7] Notorious Italian-American mobster "Lucky" Luciano is generally believed to have aided the Americans in the Allied landing in Sicily in 1943 by providing them with contacts among the local Mafia anxious to help defeat the Fascist government. A number of these mafiosi quickly regained prominence thereafter, some of them replacing the Fascist *podestà* as mayors of local governments. (t.n.)

OBSERVATIONS ON THE CHAPTERS

Chapter I

Vanni's and Vincenzo's decision to emigrate, respectively, to the United States and Argentina in order to send money back home to get their land out of hock was an intelligent move. Farm produce, in those crisis years, in fact was never enough to pay the biannual dues to the proprietor. One alternative to emigration might have been to take out a loan from a bank. But Luigi, Vanni, and Vincenzo had seen what happened in the late nineteenth century, and continued to happen in the twentieth, to so many small landowners. De Stefano and Oddo, in their *History of Sicily from 1860 to 1910* (Bari 1963), have the following to say on the matter:

"Many small properties were confiscated by the treasury for failure to pay taxes, and numerous holdings were given over to a few credit institutions for insolvency and inability to pay installments and the interests on the mortgages; and many proprietors sold their farms, after owning them for just a few years, to individuals who already owned one or more domains."

*

The Saccos are well known in Raffadali because they have never done any harm to anyone, have always respected the law, have always kept their word, and have always paid their debts. They are appreciated for their extraordinary capacity for work, and for the commitment they bring to everything they do.

All possessed of clean records, they are always granted permission to bear arms without any difficulty.

With the money they put aside, they do not buy public debt bonds, because they want to use the money to fund new initiatives, expand their activities, create work for others, and benefit their town. In the eyes of certain individuals, however, they have a flaw that is hard to ignore: they are all socialists.

Chapter II

In recent times, with the end of the bloody war declared by the Corleonese Mafia against its internal enemies and then against the state, there has been a widespread, growing reevaluation of the "old" Mafia. In reality, as this chapter amply shows, the "old" Mafia was made up of savage killers just as much as the "new" one is. The only difference between the two is that the "old" Mafia had its own deluded "code of honor." This code, however, made no allowances for either the lives or the honor of its victims, as was seen in the appalling example of the Gallo family.

Chapter III

The Dantesque language Alfonso uses to describe the conditions in which the Saccos were forced to live is quite apropos. At a certain point in their peaceful, honest, industrious lives, the Saccos are compelled to abandon utterly their habits, modes of behavior, even their way of thinking. They are forced to enter "the dark wood from which they would never manage to emerge again." But who wanted to chase them into the dark wood? Who changed the charge of their strength from positive to negative?

The Mafia, of course.

Had they bowed to the Mafia's demands, the Saccos could have continued their pursuits, while ceding a large slice of their revenues. But this big cut would have necessarily curtailed any possibility of developing their initiatives.

Moreover, the Mafia's demands would certainly have gradually grown more onerous, aggressive, and untenable, until they finally stifled all of the Saccos' pursuits.

And anyway, why passively bow one's head? Alfonso writes

that he and his brothers felt their blood boiling. Their pride as free men would not allow such cowardly submission.

But it wasn't just the Mafia that chased them into the dark wood.

They were also given a strong initial push by the marshal of the Carabinieri, when he admitted that the government was powerless. And the judges who acquitted the four defendants, taking their word, as prior convicts, against that of the law-abiding Sacco brothers who had spotless records—didn't they also push them from behind, with the law's full force, as deep into the wild wood as they could?

Chapter IV

When Salvatore Sacco manages to find out the names of those who, in trying to kill his brothers, indirectly caused his son to go blind, he doesn't go and mete out revenge personally, he lawfully files a charge with the authorities. He still has faith in the law. But how long can such faith last in the face of a law which, for the second time, chooses to take the word of former convicts and is ready to accept false evidence, even though it is fully aware that Mafia has the Saccos in their sights?

We must remember, however, that almost all these judicial procedures against the Mafia—ninety-nine percent of the time—were destined to end in the acquittal of the bosses, with minor convictions for a few subalterns. The reason for the acquittal was usually lack of evidence. And every acquittal for lack of evidence was a feather in a mafioso's cap, a medal to wear on his chest. It was a public testimony of the powerlessness of the justice system, one that conferred a kind of aura of demonic cleverness around the person of the Mafia boss, as if to say: "They just can't beat this guy."

On the other hand, the judges, even when they were not

already predisposed to leniency in the Mafia's regard—
whether for reasons of "getting along," family ties, friendships,
collusion, blackmail, or political pressure—always found
themselves, at the moment of trial, faced with legions of reluc-
tant (due to fear or convenience) or downright false witnesses.
Almost all of the alibis provided to the Mafia bosses came from
witnesses paid or suborned by the Mafia. And, as the statistics
of the time show, even acknowledged false testimonies were
usually not prosecuted. Also:

"The recalcitrant witness acts not only for or against the
interests of others, but also, and most often, for his own sake.
We see men mortally wounded who denounce their assassins,
and then, when on the road to recovery, firmly retract their
charges. We see others who denounce supposed killers instead
of the real ones—either to avenge themselves on their enemies,
or to throw law enforcement off the trail and preserve their own
or their family's honor and their obligation to take revenge."
(*Relazione della Giunta d'inchiesta parlamentare 1875* (Report
of the Parliamentary Investigation Commission, 1875), vol. II,
Bologna 1969).

Forty-five years after the abovementioned parliamentary
investigation, nothing has changed in any way.

Chapter V

Of the two versions of Vanni's escape, the one given by
Alfonso is the less convincing, though it serves in a big way to
shift the blame away from the prison authorities. In fact, for
Alfonso, it was all merely a case of negligence on the part of the
jailors, and Vanni was able to take full advantage of it. In the
other version, Vanni's getaway appears instead objectively
abetted by the entire prison hierarchy. Alfonso recounts that
his brother escaped, along with two other inmates, through a

high window left temporarily without bars. The Carabinieri say the window was out of reach. But even assuming the three men were able to reach the window, how were they able to lower themselves down on the outside, given that they were at a considerable height? With the classic bedsheets tied together? And even supposing they had found a spool of rope conveniently left by accident in their cell, would they not have been seen by some guards or passersby while descending the rope like a group of mountain climbers, since it was early afternoon? There's also another, not insignificant detail that adds to the mystery of the escape. Vanni was never officially charged with breaking out of prison. And this leads one to suspect that Vanni's escape was never reported to the proper authorities by the prison management.

But, whatever actually happened, questions remain. Who let Vanni escape, and why? It may have been someone, some powerless former victim of the Mafia, who was hoping that Vanni, once free, would resume his personal war against a common enemy, a fight that by this point, after the Saccos' father's violent death, would be without quarter. Or else it was a man of the law who, having witnessed the impossibility of fighting the Mafia legally, had decided to help it be fought illegally. And there's still another possible hypothesis. By killing an old man, namely, the Saccos' father, the Raffadalese Mafia openly and knowingly transgressed the Mafia code of honor. Indeed, by attempting to camouflage a murder by strangulation as a death by natural causes, they were hoping to evade the judgment of the other Mafias.

The attempt fails, and thus Vanni is allowed to take revenge.

Alfonso comments on Vanni's newly acquired freedom as follows:

"Was my brother's escape a good thing? Or a bad thing? I cannot judge. All the brothers on the outside were living in constant danger. After the mysterious death of our father, we knew that one or another of us might be next; whereas after our brother Giovanni's jailbreak we were all ruined, but we are all alive."

Chapter VI

History (but also crime reporting) is not made of "ifs." One cannot always resist, however, the temptation to speculate.

If the marshal of the Carabinieri, in improperly revoking Alfonso's right to bear arms, had not forced him to take to the bush (something for which he had no vocation), would the "notorious Sacco gang" have ever been born? If, in the ambush at the farmhouse, Vanni had been alone, without Alfonso at his side, would he ever have succeeded in routing the attackers? Or would he simply have been killed, and the "notorious Sacco gang" never have existed?

Whatever the case, the first two members of the "gang" are a fugitive who is not officially a fugitive, and another man who certainly cannot be defined as a fugitive because he has not been charged with any crime. At the most, Alfonso is a man who goes about armed though stripped of his license to bear arms.

The Sacco gang (which had not yet acquired that name at this point) is an utter anomaly. Because it is nothing more than the product of an accumulation of prevarications, and even a murder, contrived by mafiosi, and an intolerable string of abuses on the part of law enforcement and the justice system.

Chapter VII

There is only one witness to the Cuffaro murder, the elderly Vincenzo Galvano, who claims to have seen, right after the shot was fired, two rather young men running away. He was not able to identify them, however, because he suffers from trachomatous conjunctivitis. But his testimony is enough to put the Saccos under arrest. At the trial in 1923, the Saccos are fully acquitted of all charges. It was not merely a case of insufficient evidence.

Chapter VIII

Some time after the abortive ambush in Aragona, it was announced that the people who attacked the Saccos were either the Carabinieri or a handful of "honest and eager citizens tired of having to put up with the continuous abuses of the Sacco gang," as a newspaper put it a few years later, when recalling the episode. It goes without saying that these "honest and eager citizens" were mafiosi tried and true, who had purposefully come out in large numbers for the hunting party. How had this unusual collaboration come about? At that moment, the Raffadalese Mafia hadn't yet found a replacement for their murdered boss. But certain as they were that it was the Saccos who killed Cuffaro, they had a strong hankering for revenge. But wouldn't such a large concentration of mafiosi in Aragona have aroused the suspicions of the Carabinieri? Couldn't a police action on their part have thwarted the Mafia's plan to eliminate the Saccos? That is why they decided to inform the Carabinieri of their ambush and ally themselves with them. They were offering them the Saccos' heads on a silver platter, a prospect made possible by the treachery of the young Aragonese man. In exchange they were allowed to take part in the game.

Chapter IX

The Saccos never once opened fire on the Carabinieri or any other law enforcement officers (when they reacted to the

Aragona ambush they had no way of knowing that representatives of the law were also present). The Saccos never stole anything from anyone (the charge of stealing livestock that landed Vanni in jail proved to be patently false). Thus one wonders: what kind of "gang" is it that does not kill honest citizens, does not extort duty, commits no robbery or holdups, and never kidnaps anyone? It's a one-of-a-kind "gang" accused, and with no evidence at that, of having eliminated a few savage Mafia bosses and forced a few others to flee. It's a gang that liberated Raffadali from Mafia oppression. It's a gang of honest men forced, by events and by a government unable to protect them, to take up arms, against their very nature as honest men.

Chapter X

When informed that Mori had been sent to Sicily to fight the Mafia, noted statesman and diplomat Vittorio Emanuele Orlando, a native of Palermo, gave a famous speech at the Teatro Massimo in that same city, ending with the declaration quoted earlier in this book. Perhaps it's worth presenting a more extensive excerpt:

"Now I say to you, O fellow Palermitans, that if by the word 'Mafia' we mean a sense of honor taken to the point of paroxysm, a generosity that confronts the strong but indulges the weak, a loyalty in friendship stronger than anything, even death, if by 'Mafia' we mean these feelings and attitudes, even with all their excesses, then we are speaking of individual features that distinguish the Sicilian soul, and in that case I declare myself to be a mafioso, too, and proud to be one!"

A Mafia of fine, manly sentiment, in short. A bit the way Tryphosa Bates-Batcheller thought of it, when, in her 1911 book *Italian Castles and Country Seats*, she wrote that the origins of the Mafia were to be found "in man's primordial instinct to protect his woman."

*

The "liberation" of Gangi from the Mafia (430 arrested) was solemnly celebrated by Cesare Mori in person, who gave a speech from a balcony of the town hall to the terrorized population. Beside him was Alfredo Cucco, whom the prefect hadn't yet fingered as a mafioso, wearing the Fascist black shirt and an aviator's helmet. Mori for his part was wearing big boots and an incomprehensible, oversized light-blue band across his chest. In a powerful voice he said, among other things:

"Citizens! I will not lay down my arms. The government will not lay down its arms! You have the right to be free from riffraff, and you shall be! Our operation will be carried out through to the end, until the entire province of Palermo has been saved. The government, through my efforts, will perform its duty to the fullest, and you must do yours. You who are not afraid of rifles but fear the renown of the 'cops,' get used to the idea that the war against criminality is the duty of all honest citizens. You are beautiful people, strong and well built, with all the physical attributes of virility. You are therefore men, not sheep. Defend yourselves! Strike back!"

Defend yourselves and strike back. But isn't that what the Sacco brothers were trying to do?

Chapter XI

The intervention of the Fascist political secretary brings to light, to some extent, an element thus far kept in the background, though always present: the Saccos' political loyalties.

The Saccos never "threw themselves into politics" (as people would start to do in more recent times), but this didn't prevent all the brothers from embracing socialist ideas.

Their freedom is therefore a perpetual affront to the Fascists.

The ridicule resulting from the Saccos' escape, moreover, sparks a profound hostility towards them among the special forces who had besieged them. Capturing them becomes something more than a police operation, at this point. It's a personal matter.

The situation is paradoxical.

The Saccos liberated Raffadali from the Mafia, as Mori had exhorted Sicilians to do.

But the forces of order were against them.

The Saccos, however, had no intention of doing anything against the forces of order. At most they might reproach them for doing nothing to help them when they most needed them. Or worse.

Chapter XII

That the repressive actions taken by Mori's men in Raffadali were prompted by Commendatore V is a plausible hypothesis. This is what Alfonso Sacco maintains in the *Biography* he wrote while in Saluzzo Prison after the fall of Fascism.

But it's not possible to prove, through witnesses, the secret meeting he tells of having with Commendatore V, in the course of which the Commendatore advised the two brothers not to turn themselves in yet. What is certain is that this meeting, if it did take place, occurred only a few days before the arrival of Mori's men in Raffadali.

Chapter XIII

The savage violence of the special forces following the

surrender of the "gang" cannot be proved, though it is highly probable.

Nobody at the trial asked Lieutenant Nuvoletti how, in a firefight that lasted two hours, according to his declarations, one of the "gang" members could be killed and the other four more or less seriously wounded, without a single member of the special forces being even grazed by a bullet.

The Fascist assault on the Carabinieri compound on October 28, in an attempt to have the prisoners turned over to them, confirmed that the "notorious Sacco gang" had become a matter more of politics than public safety.

Chapter XIV

The same article by Giuseppe Pirrello contains a supplementary interview with the senator and mayor of Raffadali, Salvatore Di Benedetto.

"The townsfolk had created a legend because, among other things, they'd been won over by the fact that the Saccos were keen to have a 'style' of their own. One day, when they were staying at a house in town, they were surrounded by the Carabinieri. Vincenzo Sacco climbed up onto the roof and gave a speech trumpeting their desire for justice. After which they managed to break the encirclement and escape. They realized they had to create a consensus if they were going to hold out. And this consensus derived from the fact that they obstinately opposed the Mafia, which is, and remains, cowardly when confronted by organized forces. And that's what the Saccos were, in a way: an organized force fighting on equal terms against the Mafia. They had their own collectors in town who would go from house to house to gather funds in the name of and for use by the gang."

A "legend," says Senator Di Benedetto. But what does it mean, concretely speaking, to fight the Mafia "on equal terms"? It means shooting back at mafiosi, just as the mafiosi would shoot at anyone who didn't want to submit to their abuses.

Once freed, Alfonso agreed to a few interviews. And when they appeared in print, he would carefully correct the inaccuracies in pen, in the margins.

For Pirrello's article, where he admitted that the killing of Plano and Mangione was the work of the Saccos, he made no correction.

So maybe it wasn't all legend.

Chapter XV

The Sacco brothers always claimed they were innocent of the crimes attributed to them. And they firmly maintained this position throughout the many long years of their imprisonment, and even after they were pardoned.

But then who did kill the two Mafia bosses, Cuffaro and Terrazzino, and force the other mafiosi of Raffadali to get out of town? It is not, of course, up to the Saccos to furnish the names of the real culprits.

One hypothesis of which Alfonso allows a glimpse, however, is that the two murders were either the result of an internal feud, or were committed by someone who was fed up with the Mafia's abuse and took matters into his own hands, knowing that the killings would in any case be blamed on the Sacco brothers. The Saccos claimed they limited themselves to demonstrative actions, such as scaring to death the lawyer who functioned as the brains of the Mafia.

To tell the truth, one cannot say that the Saccos' last trial, the definitive one, unfolded in an atmosphere of serenity and balance. And so?

So the Saccos everyone knew as solitary avengers, infallible sharpshooters, and tireless, unconquerable fighters were merely a town legend?

And the Mafia was defeated by three nonexistent knights?

By empty suits of armor?

By simple appearances?

If so, then what an amazing story!

Author's Note

I've been able to tell this utterly true story only because Giovanni Sacco, one of Girolamo's six children, asked me to recount the vicissitudes his family lived through, and provided me with official documents, family writings and correspondences, and minutes of the trials.

I would therefore like to thank him with all my heart and dedicate this book to his memory.

I've limited myself only to changing a name or two here and there and using false initials.

I have tried to show, through this "Western of things of ours"[8]—to use one of Sciascia's titles—how the Mafia not only kills, but in those cases where the state goes missing, is also able to shape and irreparably upend people's lives.

A.C.

---

[8] The Italian original of this phrase, *Western di cose nostre,* plays of course on one of the names by which the Mafia is known in Italian, *la cosa nostra,* "this thing of ours." (t.n.)